Praise for
Fairy Tale in New York

'An absolutely incredible, yet authentic, fairy tale adventure.
Wonderfully "feel good" for the holiday season.'
~ Jessie Dalrymple

'Highly recommended to brighten your spirits and fall head first
into a modern fairy tale.'
~ JB Johnston at Brook Cottage Books Blog

'Fairy Tale in New York is an uplifting, festive, feel-good novella
that restores faith in hope and humanity. The perfect Christmas
read!' ~ Kelly at Perusing Princesses Blog

NICKY WELLS

Fairy Tale in New York

How do you celebrate Christmas with no place to stay, no food, and no presents?

Nicky Wells
http://nickywells.com/

First paperback edition printed by
CreateSpace Independent Publishing Platform, November 2014:
ISBN-13: 978-1501044700
ISBN-10: 1501044702

Author photograph by Deborah Smith

Cover design: Nicky Wells

Cover image: © Dreamstimer99 | Dreamstime.com — New York Skyline And Central Park After Snow Storm Photo

A British Novella with British Spellings

Hello! Here are my customary musings on spelling: British versus American English.

'Fairy Tale in New York' presents me with a bit of a conundrum. On the one hand, the main characters — Jude and Carrie — are very much British. On the other hand, this book is set entirely in New York. What is a writer who is clearly prone to making her life unnecessarily complicated to do?

After much debate with myself, my patient husband, a focus group of British *and* North American readers, as well as my (British and North American) beta-readers, I decided to stick with the British voice for the characters. Therefore, my North American audience will find that the characters in this story like *colours*, proceed with *honour*, make *judgements*, *apologise*, and resist *generalisations*. They *travelled*, *dialled* and *marvelled*. Their cars have *tyres*, and the roads are divided from *pavements* (rather than sidewalks) by *kerbs* (not curbs). The list goes on, but I hope you'll enjoy the ride despite these strange spellings and the occasional unfamiliar expression! Thank you, as always, for bearing with me. Rock on!

~ 1 ~

Stay Another Day

'I can't believe it's all over. Where did three weeks go?'

Carrie smiled at Jude while shifting their baby daughter, Maya, onto her other hip. The check-in queue at JFK airport had ground to a complete standstill, and Carrie was beginning to struggle with her six-month-old's weight. Unperturbed, Maya gurgled happily and snuggled her head onto Carrie's shoulder.

'She's half asleep again,' Jude commented and stroked his daughter's rosy cheeks. He planted a quick kiss on Carrie's forehead before responding to her question.

'It's crazy, isn't it? Three weeks on tour all over the US, and suddenly it's done. Seventeen gigs in twenty-one days. My God, I'm not half knackered.'

'It was worth it, though. You were a runaway success.' Carrie grinned with proprietorial pride at her rock star boyfriend. 'They loved you.'

Jude chuckled. 'They did, too, didn't they? Gosh, San Francisco was a riot. I thought they'd take the stage down.'

'I've never seen so much underwear flying your way. You're gonna have to watch it, mate, or your girlfriend might get the wrong idea,' Carrie teased.

'Oh no, she won't. She knows I love her.'

Jude looked Carrie deep in the eyes. He hoped she knew how much he loved her. One of these days, he ought to make an honest woman out of her. He had planned to, of course. He even had a ring. But what with Carrie having fallen pregnant, she hadn't wanted to get married before the baby was born. 'I don't want to *waddle* down the aisle,' she had joked when they had talked about it almost a year ago now. 'I want to *float*, serenely.'

Add the band's recording deal and the UK and European tours into the mix of their crazy life, and there hadn't been the right time. There hadn't been *any* time. They had just about managed to furnish a nursery for Maya, but that had been it on the family front.

New Year's Eve, Jude resolved silently. *I'll propose to her then, and we'll marry in the summer.*

He snapped to abruptly when he realised Carrie was still talking.

'I think Dan was a little put out at not getting quite so much attention himself after you gave up the stage,' she was saying.

Dan was the mentor, manager, and record label owner behind Jude's band, The Blood Roses, and also the lead singer of his own band, Tuscq. He was now on his way to Toronto for a special Christmas Eve show.

'Dan was fine. He's thrilled that it's going so well for us. And *I* am looking forward to a lovely quiet Christmas at home, just me and my girls.'

Jude wrapped Carrie and the now sleeping Maya into a hug. The Blood Roses weren't opening for Tuscq for the Toronto gig and had therefore gone their separate ways. Jude and Carrie elected to go back to London straightaway, but the rest of the band had added a short trip to Las Vegas to their itinerary.

'Home. Ha. If we ever get there,' Carrie grumbled. She yawned widely. It was only five-thirty a.m. Their flight to London Heathrow was due to leave in a little over two hours, but the queue hadn't advanced for at least fifteen minutes. 'Here, can you hold Maya a minute? She's getting rather heavy.'

Jude took the baby out of Carrie's arms and rocked her contentedly. He hadn't expected to become so utterly bewitched by a toothless, hairless, and demanding little being.

Quite suddenly, the distant babble of voices that had been permeating his consciousness rose to a shouted exchange. Jude turned towards the front of the queue, curious to see what the commotion might be.

'I really, really need to get on this flight,' a harassed-looking man in an expensive suit reiterated. He wiped his brow with a monogrammed white handkerchief and tapped his fingers on the counter impatiently. Jude couldn't help but eavesdrop along with the rest of the terminal.

'Look,' the man continued, adopting a more reasonable tone. 'I know I'm not booked on this flight. But tomorrow is too late for me. I'm willing to pay anything at all to get a seat, any class. First class, cattle class, I really don't care. I need to get home.'

'Yeah, you and the rest of us,' Carrie whispered softly next to Jude. Jude didn't react. He was mesmerised by the scene unfolding before him. He had half expected the man to lose his temper and for airport security to step in and escort him away. However, instead there were deep breaths and a beseeching voice.

'My wife's in labour,' the man explained. He was speaking more or less to the entire queue by now. 'I just had word. The baby is five weeks early. I really have to get back, can't you see? If I could only get on this flight…'

He didn't finish his plea but looked at the airline employee with hopeful eyes.

'Sir, I'm really sorry.' The clerk's voice was calm and filled with regret. 'I'd like to help, but this flight is full. If you want to try another airline, perhaps…'

'I've tried all the airlines. All the flights are full. It's the twenty-third of December. Everybody and their mother is travelling.' He paused to compose himself and continued in a more measured voice again. 'Besides, this is the soonest flight. I really need to get home. I can't let her go through this on her own.'

Jude was aware that Carrie was holding his hand and squeezing it tightly. 'You okay?' she whispered.

Jude nodded and swallowed hard. The man's distress brought back to him vivid memories of Maya's birth.

Maya hadn't been early; on the contrary, she had taken her sweet time. When she was a week past her due date, The Blood Roses were scheduled for a promotional gig in Manchester. The date had been set months previously and was immovable. Jude flew up from London at the last moment and was booked to return that same night, foregoing the after-party and the TV interview.

Of course, Carrie went into labour while he was on stage. Luckily, his travel arrangements worked out, and Jude had joined Carrie in the hospital to help her through the last twelve hours of giving birth.

Nonetheless, the flight back from Manchester to London had been the longest journey of his life. He remembered all too clearly the worry, the anxiety, the sense of powerlessness, and the desperate need to be with Carrie. Expensive-suit man at the front of the queue was evidently going through the same range of emotions, most likely amplified tenfold given the sheer distance he had to cover.

'I'll swap you.'

Jude spoke before he realised what he was doing. He hoisted Maya higher in his arms and stepped forward, pulling Carrie along by the hand. The man stared at him in wonderment.

'You can have my flight,' Jude clarified, speaking more confidently now that his idea had taken proper shape in his head. 'And I'll take yours tomorrow.'

'But Jude,' Carrie piped up from his side. 'What about Maya and me?'

'You take your flight, and I'll see you tomorrow.'

'Oh lordy...' Carrie's voice clearly told of her panic. 'I don't know if I can cope on my own, with Maya and all, on a long flight...'

'You can, honey, I know you can. Or else you could stay here, and I'll take Maya with me today. Either way, we've got to get this man home. It's important.'

The man cleared his throat. 'Are you… are you sure? I don't want to disrupt your family… I mean, I'd absolutely love to pick you up on your offer, but…' He shrugged helplessly, almost defeated.

Jude, Carrie, and the man stood in a tight circle in front of the check-in desk. Impatient grumbling behind them suggested that the other waiting passengers weren't best pleased about the new development.

'I'm sure we can sort this out. Let's see if the lady here can help us swap flights, first of all.'

Jude was all calm determination. He placed his and Carrie's tickets on the counter for the check-in clerk to examine.

'It'll be all right,' he whispered into Carrie's ear while the clerk got busy at her computer. 'You wouldn't have wanted me to miss Maya's birth, would you?'

Carrie shuddered. 'Of course not. But…'

'No buts. It'll be fine. It's only a day…'

'I'm the duty manager. Can I help at all?' A fresh voice entered the conversation. Another frustrated groan arose from the waiting passengers, but Jude and expensive-suit man paid no attention.

The airline clerk swiftly summarised the situation. 'So Mr Shaw here'—she smiled at Jude when she said his name—'has kindly agreed to exchange flights with Mr Whyte…'

'I'll pay any rebooking fees, of course,' expensive suit interjected hastily. Jude inclined his head to acknowledge the offer but said nothing.

'Hmm...' The manager rubbed his chin. 'Let's see here.' He tapped at the keyboard and consulted a few screens.

'What about Mrs Shaw?' he asked.

'Miss Collins,' Carrie corrected automatically. 'I'll fly back with our daughter today.'

'Hmm.' The manager rubbed his chin once more. 'What would you say if I could rebook your flight as well, so that you can return to London with your partner tomorrow?'

'Um, yes. Well... I...' Carrie was flustered by the development.

Mr Whyte laughed delightedly. 'That would be amazing.'

'But what would we do? Where would we stay?'

'Easy.' Mr Whyte looked more relaxed by the second as he worked out the details of the plan. 'I have a hotel room booked in the city for tonight. I wasn't supposed to go home today, remember? You can have it. For free.'

Carrie opened her mouth to protest, but Mr Whyte spoke regardless. 'Look, it's the least I can do. It's all paid for anyway. If you don't take it, it'll be empty tonight. So you might as well. It's plenty big for the three of you. I'll call them and change the reservation as soon as we're done here.'

'Let's do it,' Jude cut to the chase, speaking directly to the duty manager. 'If you can swap mine and Mr Whyte's flights around and book Carrie onto the same plane as me tomorrow...'

'What about Maya? Will there be an infant seat available for her?' She hesitated, unwilling to be an obstacle at the last minute. 'Doesn't matter. She can travel on our laps.'

'Don't worry, we'll make it happen,' the manager assured her. 'Let me swap your reservations.'

'I'll pay the fees,' Mr Whyte repeated.

'That won't be necessary,' the manager replied. 'This is an emergency. Besides, you're a platinum card holder.'

Jude nudged Carrie and winked. 'A platinum card holder. That explains a lot,' he breathed into her ear. 'One day, I want to be a platinum card holder.'

'And so you shall,' Carrie whispered back. 'Now we've an extra day in New York. What'll we do?'

'We'll put it to good use,' Jude promised her. 'It'll be magical. And tomorrow we'll fly home for Christmas.'

'Right,' the manager cut into Jude and Carrie's muted exchange. 'That's all sorted. One new set of tickets for Mr Shaw and Miss Collins…and one new ticket for Mr Whyte. Mr Whyte, you ought to be making your way through security soon. Is there anything else I can do for you today?'

'You've done plenty, thank you.' Mr Whyte extended a hand to the manager. 'This is rock star service. Thank you again. And you…'

He turned to Jude and Carrie. 'What's your name again?'

'Jude Shaw,' Jude introduced himself. 'And my partner, Carrie Collins. Our daughter, Maya.'

'Jude Shaw,' Mr Whyte mused and scrutinised Jude closely. 'You look familiar. 'Do I know you?'

Jude shook his head. 'I don't think so.'

'Are you sure?'

Jude shrugged. Mr Whyte gave him another intense look but let the matter go. Instead, he picked up his mobile phone and made a quick call. He made a 'let's walk' gesture and ambled away from the check-in desk to make way for the passengers still waiting in line. Jude and Carrie followed along, Carrie once again carrying Maya and Jude pushing the trolley with their luggage.

After a few steps, Mr Whyte stopped and held up a hand while he continued talking into his mobile phone.

'Yes, that's right. Mr Shaw and Miss Collins, plus baby Maya. For tonight. Yes. I want you to take good care of them for me. Great. Thanks.'

He clicked off the call and smiled widely at Jude and Carrie. 'Sorted. The transfer car is waiting outside for you and will take you straight to the hotel. I won't forget this, you know.'

'I'm sure you won't,' Jude laughed. 'I was on a flight, too, when Carrie went into labour. It was only a short hop but man, it seemed to take forever. I'll never forget. Good luck to you and your wife. I hope the baby is all right.'

'So do I, so do I.' A shadow of concern flitted over Mr Whyte's face, and he stroked his forehead wearily. 'Five weeks early…'

'It'll be okay,' Carrie spoke up. 'Five weeks is premature, but it *is* near term. They'll take good care of him or her in the hospital, I'm sure.'

'Thanks,' Mr Whyte replied. 'I hope so. We've been waiting for this baby a long time.' He smiled wistfully. 'Well, I best be off, or this flight will leave without me after all. I wish you a safe trip tomorrow, and thank you again for all your troubles. God bless.'

'Off you go,' Jude smiled and made a jokey shooing gesture with his hands. Mr Whyte turned and walked away, throwing them a backward wave as he went.

'What an unexpected turn of events.' Carrie was momentarily stunned. She wrapped her free arm around Jude's waist and kissed him on the mouth. 'You're a kind man, Jude Shaw. That was a wonderful thing to do, even if I was a bit worried at first.'

Jude lifted his shoulders and cocked his head. He didn't quite know how to respond to Carrie's praise. Last Christmas, he had been on the brink of losing everything, and he had been anything but a 'kind man' back then. If it hadn't been for those extraordinary events of last Christmas Eve, he wouldn't be standing here with Carrie and his daughter. Nor would he ever have considered helping someone else in quite such a radical fashion.

'Let's go find that transfer car,' he said gruffly, trying to conceal his emotions. 'Let's hope Mr Whyte had a fairly nice hotel in mind for himself.'

'Oh, I should think so,' Carrie giggled. 'Did you see his suit? That must have cost a small fortune.'

'Certainly did. Let's see if his hotel is equally exquisite.'

'Where are you taking us?' Jude asked the driver as they were cruising back into New York City. 'Somewhere nice?'

'You don't know?' the driver asked, incredulous. He half turned to examine Jude, Carrie, and Maya huddled in the back seat of his limousine.

'No, we don't,' Carrie explained. 'It was kind of a last minute thing.'

'But you are Mr Whyte's guests, yes?'

'Oh yes,' Jude confirmed quickly. 'But he only told us it's a hotel in the city.'

'That's Mr Whyte all over,' the driver confirmed wryly. 'Well, you're sure to have a nice surprise. I won't be saying anything more, apart from... Park Avenue.'

'Park Avenue?' Carrie was aghast. 'That sounds expensive,' she whispered to Jude.

'Who cares?' he whispered back. 'It's all paid for, he said.'

Maya babbled and made a grab for Carrie's hair. She had just woken after her unscheduled nap in the airport and was sitting on Carrie's lap regarding her environment with curious eyes. Carrie took her daughter's fist and pretended to eat it. Maya squealed with delight. Jude smiled.

'It's an adventure,' he suggested. 'For all of us. Hey...um... Excuse me?' He tried to get the driver's attention. 'What would you do with your young family if you happened to have a random unexpected day in New York City?'

The driver tapped his fingers on the steering wheel. 'With a young one? In this cold weather? Lemme think...' He waggled his head from side to side

'Yeah, here goes. Why don't you all take the sightseeing tour? It's nice and cosy on the bus, and you can get off whenever you want...'

'Hm. Not a bad idea, thank you,' Jude replied. 'I quite fancy doing the touristy thing. I never get to do that anymore.'

'And here you are,' the driver announced suddenly, pulling up in front of one of the world's most famous hotels.

Carrie gasped. 'You're kidding me!'

The driver chuckled. 'Didn't I know you were gonna love this surprise?'

'Is this for real?' Carrie persisted. 'You're not pulling our legs?'

'No, ma'am. This is for real.'

'Oh. My. God.'

The driver jumped out and opened Carrie's door before Jude could quite absorb what was happening. Jude scrabbled to get out too, straightening up and casting an incredulous look at the iconic building familiar to him from dozens and dozens of movies.

'Well, well, well,' he muttered. 'I'll be damned.'

A bellhop arrived to take their luggage, and the driver hopped back into his car and drove off without giving Jude the chance to mutter so much as a 'thank you.'

Jude looked after him and shook his head. 'Weird,' he muttered under his breath. He turned to Carrie, who was already climbing up the few steps towards the entrance doors. 'Shall I carry Maya for you?'

'No, thanks. I feel totally underdressed for this place, and at least Maya will cover some of my sins.'

Jude grinned. 'Will she now?'

'Shush, you.' Carrie nudged her boyfriend with an elbow, and he nudged her back affectionately. The hotel doorman doffed his cap and greeted them warmly, opening the door as they entered the lobby and faced a breathtaking vista. Marble floors, high ceilings, wood panelling, gilded elevator doors… Artwork, flowers, elegant sofas, even a miniature Statue of Liberty. A majestic Christmas tree graced the centre of the hall, trimmed elegantly with silver and white baubles, sparkling stars, icicles, and a tasteful dusting of fake snow.

'This is a different world,' Carrie breathed.

'Who knows? One day it might be ours,' Jude offered loftily.

'You'll have to sell a hell of a lot of records before this is our world,' Carrie scoffed in a good-natured way.

'Oh ye of little faith,' Jude admonished. 'Let's go and find out where our room is.'

'Ah, Mr Shaw. Miss Collins.' The receptionist behind the lavish counter appeared to have been expecting them. She smiled at Maya and tapped at her keyboard to print out a check-in form.

'It's all done for you,' she explained as she pushed the form towards Jude. 'All you have to do is sign.'

Jude took the pen and got poised to write, then paused and blanched.

'Is everything all right, sir?'

'Yes. Of course. Only…' Jude angled the paper so that Carrie could see. 'It says here that we'll be staying in a suite?'

'That's right,' the receptionist confirmed cheerfully. 'It's Mr Whyte's favourite. He always stays in the Cooper Suite. He says it inspires him.'

'*The Cooper Suite?*' Carrie mouthed at Jude.

Jude shrugged and nodded at the same time. 'I guess so.' He scribbled his name and returned the form to the receptionist. She gave him a key card in return.

'There you go, sir. Your suite is on the thirtieth floor. The bellhop will be taking your luggage up for you. I hope you enjoy your stay.'

She smiled, and Jude began to turn away. At the last moment, she called out to him once more.

'Sir?'

'Yes?'

'Sir, I gather you may not have had breakfast. Would you like to order some breakfast to be delivered to your rooms?'

'Um… Would we, Carrie?' Jude shot his girlfriend a quick amused look.

'Oh, yes please,' Carrie agreed. 'That would be lovely.'

'What would you like, ma'am?'

Carrie shrugged helplessly, and Jude ordered on her behalf. 'Would it be possible to get a selection of things on your standard breakfast menu? Some rolls, maybe, or pancakes, and some preserves? We're not fussy, only starved.'

The receptionist smiled. 'We can certainly do that, sir. I'll have room service bring your breakfast in a few minutes.'

Jude and Carrie took the elevator to the thirtieth floor, where they stepped out into a quiet, thickly carpeted corridor with antique paintings on the wall and dainty side tables bearing vases of flowers.

'Wow. It's a little different from the hotels on tour,' Carrie exclaimed.

'Certainly is. Look…' Jude had spied a discrete sign pointing down the corridor towards the Cooper Suite. 'We're that way.'

Together, they walked to the suite. Carrie still held Maya, so Jude inserted the key card and opened the door. They entered into a lobby, and immediately the door closed behind them with a soft clunk. They took a moment to absorb the ambience and walked through into a reception room featuring a sumptuous sofa suite, a grand piano, floor-length curtains, and more rich detail than Jude could take in all at once. Tiny white Christmas lights had been arranged in vases and tastefully strung along picture frames and windows, and one corner of the room even sported a smaller version of the grand tree from the lobby.

Baby Maya appeared uninterested in the delights of the suite. She wriggled in Carrie's arms, and Carrie bent down to set her gently onto the thick rug in the middle of the room. Maya cooed happily. Carrie surveyed her surroundings some more. She ran a hand through her hair and half laughed, half choked.

'Oh my God, Jude, this is a palace. Who *is* Mr Whyte that he stays here?'

Jude had taken a seat on one of the sofas. He grinned at Carrie. 'I've no idea. And frankly, m'dear, I don't give a damn. This is quite something. It's like we won the lottery.'

'It's like a dream,' Carrie agreed. 'A fairy tale. Let's hope there's no evil witch coming after us. I'll go and check in the closets…'

She grinned and left the reception room to explore the rest of the suite. Jude remained on the sofa, keeping an eye on Maya and listening with amusement to Carrie's shouts of glee as she relayed discovery after discovery to him.

'Jude, the bed… It's massive! And…' A thump and a squeal indicated that Carrie had thrown herself bodily on the bed. 'It's so soft! *And* they put up a cot for Maya…. Right… There's the bathroom, and it's all marble and gold plated taps…sorry, faucets they are, of course…and…'

Jude saw Carrie cross the foyer and disappear into a room on the other side. 'Oh my gosh, there's a dining room that's like… It's a boardroom, you could host the UN in here, and there's a kitchen, too. I mean, a real, actual kitchen, fridge, hob and all. This place is unbelievable.'

Carrie joined Jude in the reception room once more and flopped on the sofa opposite him. 'What say we stay here and never move out?'

Jude suppressed a snort. 'As you say, darling, when I've sold enough records, we can talk about that…'

There was a knock on the door.

'That'll be our breakfast or our luggage,' Carrie speculated and raced off to open the door. Jude smiled at her obvious excitement.

It was indeed their breakfast *and* their luggage. For a few moments, there was a flurry of activity as a waiter pushed a trolley of breakfast dishes into the reception room and the bellhop deposited their luggage in the bedroom. Both men duly tipped, they departed and left Jude and Carrie in stunned bewilderment once more. Then hunger took over, and Jude lifted the silver domes covering their breakfast dishes.

By nine a.m., the little family had feasted royally, showered, and dressed again. After a quick call to Jude's and

Carrie's parents with an update on their situation, they were ready to be let loose on New York City. They emerged onto Park Avenue to find a bright blue sky with a low, watery sun just visible among the towering skyscrapers.

The concierge had suggested catching the 'Downtown' tour outside Rockefeller Center, so Jude and Carrie directed their feet there. Jude carried Maya in a sling in front of his chest, as had become his wont during the band's US tour.

For rest of the day, the trio played at being tourists in New York City. They visited Times Square, journeyed to the top of the Empire State Building, took photos of the Statue of Liberty and the World Trade Center Memorial, marvelled at the sheer amount of taxis that turned the streets into a sea of yellow, and had a walk around Little Italy. All through the day, they admired the staggering amounts of seasonal lights and larger-than-life decorations all over the city.

'It's like the *National Lampoon's Christmas Vacation*,' Carrie laughed when she spotted the eighty-foot tree at Rockefeller Center. 'I bet you can see this from space.'

'You can see New York City from space at any time,' Jude teased her mildly. 'But I know what you mean. I love it too, even if it is, you know, a bit much.'

'Grinch,' Carrie admonished and nudged him in the side.

They put in pit stops for Maya at various department stores, and at one point, Jude thought he would never manage to get Carrie to leave Macy's. In the early afternoon, they took lunch in a coffee shop where Maya grabbed a nap on one of the banquette seats and allowed Jude and Carrie to have an hour's adult conversation. Later, they had an early dinner near their hotel in a 'real, bona-fide American diner,' as Carrie shouted gleefully, where they ordered burgers, fries, and milkshakes and put quarter after quarter into the little table-top jukebox. Maya dined on milk and little morsels of sweet pancake.

'This is totally magical,' Carrie repeated for the umpteenth time while they waited to pay for their meal. 'It's been absolutely fantastic, but now I'm done in. And so is our little princess.'

She planted a light kiss on her daughter's droopy head. 'I think it might be time to go home.'

Jude stretched his hands above his head and suppressed a yawn. 'We had a massively early start, and we've been on our feet more or less all day. No wonder we're tired. But man, what a gift.' He grinned.

'I know. I can't believe we've done a lightning tour of the Big Apple. It's totally unreal. I feel very lucky. It's all so romantic!'

'I was hoping to get *romantic* later.' Jude grinned winningly and winked. 'Unless you're too tired, of course.'

'Mmmmh.' Carrie pretended to think this over. 'Too tired, definitely. You'll have to convince me.'

'Is that so?' Jude's eyes sparkled with the challenge. 'And how would I do that?'

'You know there's a grand piano in the lounge, right?'

'Yeah. And?'

'Well.' Carrie blushed.

'What?'

'Um.' Carrie leaned forward and dropped her voice to a whisper. 'You know that scene in *Pretty Woman*? In the bar? I've always wanted to try that out.'

Jude burst out laughing, startling Maya. 'Sorry, babycakes, I didn't mean to frighten you,' he cooed and scooped her onto his lap. 'Your mummy is propositioning me in the most outrageous manner, you know. Quite scandalous.'

'Shush,' Carrie hissed. 'What if she understands you?'

'She won't,' Jude replied calmly. 'How could she?'

'You know what they say about not talking to your baby in a baby voice…'

'Well, I'm right on track, aren't I?' Jude replied mischievously. 'As for your proposition…well, I must say… you're on. I suppose we'd better get this young lady tucked up first, don't you?'

Carrie chuckled. 'Are we naughty, or what?'

'Not naughty,' Jude corrected gently. 'Just in love. Let's go.'

He stepped up to the counter to pay at the till while Carrie put Maya back into her coat and hat. The little girl was droopy and tired and glared at Carrie around a thumb plugged firmly into her mouth. Carrie kissed her nose and tugged her hat down a little further. 'Nearly time for your bath and bed,' she told her daughter. 'It's not far to the hotel.'

Jude lifted Maya into her sling and fastened it securely. He gave a quick nod towards the window. 'Have you noticed? It's snowing.'

'Really?' Carrie squealed and pressed her nose to the window like a small child. 'Omigod, so it is! Could this day end any more perfect?'

'I don't know about perfect,' Jude grumbled. 'Let's hope it's a temporary flurry.'

'Oh, I'm sure it will be,' Carrie mused. 'You know me and snow. It never snows where I am. And if it does, it doesn't stick. But it's so romantic. Just think, we could light some candles and sit at the piano together and watch the snow fall onto Park Avenue…maybe have a glass of vino…'

'Is that before or after we try that scene from Pretty Woman?'

'You and your one-track mind.' Carrie pretended to pout and threw a glove at Jude.

'Hey, that's not fair!' Jude caught the glove and laughed. 'You suggested it.'

'That was before!'

'Before what?'

'Before it snowed!'

Jude shook with laughter all over. 'How does that change anything?'

'Well, you know.' Carrie wrapped her scarf around her neck and donned her own woolly hat. 'I never get to sit in a suite in a glamorous hotel and watch the snow fall, so that's pretty special, don't you see? I've got to *enjoy* this moment.'

'And so you shall. Just as soon as we've both enjoyed something else.'

'Tsk. Honestly. Anyone would think you're a rock star, the way you carry on.'

Carrie linked her arm into Jude's and smiled. This was one of their favourite exchanges, and they never tired of playing it out.

'I'll rock you hard,' Jude delivered his obligatory final line and grinned. He wrapped his arms around his girlfriend, encircling her in his arms around the warm bulk of baby Maya between them.

'You know you'll have to stop this saucy talk sooner or later, don't you?' Carrie couldn't resist pointing out. She cast a quick look at her daughter sandwiched snugly in between herself and Jude. 'Before too long, she *will* understand what we say.'

'We've got some time yet, my sweet. C'mon, let's brave the snow.'

They left the diner and walked along Third Avenue to return to the hotel.

It was indeed snowing. Small, wispy flakes floated on the air and settled gently on Jude's and Carrie's coats and hats. There was a chill in the air, and their breath hung in front of their mouths like little puffs of frozen steam. But the city noises of car tyres and horns, busses and trucks continued unabated despite the wintery shower, and Jude and Carrie arrived at their hotel in high spirits and with grand plans for a luxurious romantic night in.

'And tomorrow, we fly home for Christmas,' Carrie whispered contentedly before she fell asleep a few hours later.

'Tomorrow, we fly home,' Jude repeated.

~ 2 ~

Let It Snow

Jude rose at five a.m. and padded softly over to the window overlooking Park Avenue. Evidently, it had snowed all through the night. A thick blanket of snow covered the wide pavements — the *sidewalks*, Jude mentally corrected himself — and even the road surface itself was fully covered. The few cars that were about at this early hour were driving slowly, and their tyres didn't penetrate through the snow onto the black tarmac beyond. It was most extraordinary.

Even though it was still dark, the street seemed to be glowing eerily from within itself as the snow reflected the light from the streetlamps. It was a silent, cold, and magical scene. Jude shivered in his pyjamas.

'Let's hope we get to the airport,' he pleaded with fate. 'At least it's no longer snowing. It looks as if the roads are still passable, but who knows.'

He abandoned his position by the window and went into the bathroom to have a shower and shave. The previous evening, he had asked the concierge to arrange for a car to pick them up in the morning, and it was due in less than forty minutes. He worried whether perhaps he ought to try and summon it sooner. A gentle knock interrupted his musings.

'Room service,' a muted voice announced as Jude opened the door.

'Wow. Good morning,' Jude whispered while opening the door wide enough for the waiter to push in a trolley. 'You're earlier than I expected.'

'I know, sir. With apologies. We've taken the liberty of asking the car service to send your car a half hour earlier so you make it to the airport in time. The roads should be clear, but you can't be certain. And the forecast isn't good.'

The waiter spoke in hushed tones, aware now that the rest of Jude's party was still asleep. 'I hope you don't mind, sir, we thought it would be prudent.'

'Of course I don't mind. I'd been wondering about doing that myself,' Jude explained, aware that he was sounding slightly incoherent. 'I'll wake the family now. When will the car be here?'

'In about fifteen minutes, I should think.'

'Better get my skates on,' Jude joked and tipped the waiter. 'We'll be down as soon as possible.'

Jude threw on his clothes and switched on the lights in the bedroom. Carrie groaned in protest, but Maya didn't stir.

'Sweetheart. Carrie, my love. We've got to get up now.'

He poured a cup of coffee and put it on her bedside table. The sweet, strong scent of Italian espresso was enough to rouse the dead, and Carrie sat up bleary-eyed. She cast a glance at her wristwatch and sighed.

'It's only ten past five.' She gave a wide yawn and rubbed her eyes. 'I thought the car wasn't due until six.'

'It wasn't, but it snowed through the night, and the concierge decided we'd need to allow more time to get to the airport.'

'Ah.' Carrie took a sip of her coffee. She didn't comment on Jude's statement for a second, and Jude was beginning to think she hadn't understood. Then suddenly, her eyes flew wide open.

'You mean, the car will be here in ten minutes?'

'Or thereabouts.'

'Sugar!' She jumped out of bed with both feet, staggered, and sat down again. 'Why didn't you tell me before?'

'I only just found out. Don't panic.' Jude adopted his most soothing voice. 'Get dressed and grab a bite to eat while you do, and I'll take care of Maya. Thank goodness we sorted the cases last night. We'll be okay.'

'Just get dressed?' Carrie repeated, sounding incredulous. 'In ten minutes? There's make-up to be done and all sorts… I'll never make it.'

'Just get dressed,' Jude reiterated patiently. He knew his girlfriend all too well. 'You can put on your make-up in the car. It won't be going very fast, I can guarantee you that. You'll have an hour to make yourself presentable. At least.' He grimaced and corrected himself. 'Not that you're not presentable *au naturel*, but…'

Carrie threw a pillow at him. 'You're incorrigible.'

'But practical. Do you want to get this flight and celebrate Christmas at home—our daughter's first Christmas, no less?'

'Of course I do. I'll be dressed in five.'

Fifteen minutes later, Jude and Carrie emerged into the lobby carrying their luggage and baby Maya between them. The lobby was deserted except for the concierge, a bellhop, and a man dressed in a thick coat, scarf, gloves, and a woolly beret. The Christmas tree sparkled merrily, reminding Jude that it was indeed Christmas Eve.

'Please let us get home,' he prayed silently. 'Please make it happen.'

The man loitering about near the reception desk turned out to be their driver.

'Morning,' he greeted cheerfully while the bellhop took the luggage off Jude. 'Let's see if we can't get you to JFK on time. London, you're going to, is that right?' His words tumbled out in a leisurely drawl, and Jude merely nodded.

'Awesome,' the driver commented. 'I'm sure I'll get you to the airport, but whether you'll all be getting on a plane today remains to be seen.'

'What do you mean?' Carrie asked for clarification, slightly out of breath from trying to match the man's energetic pace whilst carrying Maya and her handbag.

The driver ploughed on without a backwards glance. 'There's talk of a white-out. The airport's still open for now, but who knows?'

He yanked open the boot of the car and allowed the bellhop to dump the luggage inside. 'Anything else for the trunk?' he enquired cheerfully. 'Your handbag, ma'am? The baby? *Just* kidding.' He slammed the boot shut and installed himself behind the steering wheel. 'Ready? Here we go.'

Jude and Carrie tumbled into the backseat. Jude strapped Maya into the courtesy baby seat. Once she was settled, he leaned across to give her her morning milk. His daughter hadn't been terribly impressed about being lifted from her cot and manhandled into day clothes, but she had calmed down eventually, and Jude intended to keep her that way. Meanwhile, Carrie fumbled in her handbag for her make-up essentials before the cab had even pulled away from the kerb.

As the car trundled and slid along the snowy roads, she applied moisturiser and foundation, muttering to herself all the time. Jude watched her with wry amusement. The lengths a lady would go to for her appearance always astounded him, especially if, like Carrie, she possessed a natural, glowing beauty. But he refrained from commenting and even held up his mobile phone like a little torch with his free hand so that Carrie could attempt to do her eyeliner.

'It's no good,' she sighed after she had nearly stabbed herself in the eye for the fifth time. 'Every time I'm poised, the car slips or swerves. I'll have to do this at the airport.'

'You look fine,' Jude finally reassured her. 'With or without eyeliner. I love you.'

'I love you too,' Carrie responded as she leaned back in the seat and surveyed the snowy cityscape outside. 'How's my lovely getting on with her breakfast?'

'Drained it,' Jude observed and held up the empty bottle for Carrie to see.

'Gosh. Well, she'll be all over the place today,' Carrie surmised. 'That'll be fun.'

'We'll ride it out,' Jude soothed her. 'A day out of routine won't kill her. We'll go with the flow. She's been brilliant all through the tour, she'll get through this last day of travelling, too.'

'It's gonna be a long one.'

'But at the end of it, it's Christmas,' Jude replied. He wasn't going to let Carrie's worries undermine his optimism. 'It'll be great. We'll talk about this forever.' He adopted a jittery old man's voice. 'Do you remember Maya's first Christmas when we were flying back from New York, and it had snowed all night, and the plane nearly didn't go?'

'Don't even go there,' Carrie protested, sounding panicked. 'What if it doesn't?'

'It will,' Jude assured her in his normal voice. 'We'd have heard something if it didn't.'

'I hope you're right.'

'So do I, man,' the driver chimed in ominously from the front. 'This ain't lookin' too good.'

'This what?' Jude challenged. 'You can't know what it's like at the airport?'

'No, you're right. But it *is* snowing again. It's that white-out, I'm tellin' you.'

Jude and Carrie looked out of the windows. They were crossing a bridge, and the East River looked dark and gloomy, flowing sluggishly in between snow-covered banks. Snow was once again falling thick and fast, and it seemed to be getting heavier as the cab made its way over the bridge.

'White-out?' Carrie said to Jude. 'What's he talking about?'

'The concierge said something about a bad storm being forecast,' Jude explained quietly, trying not to frighten his girlfriend. 'But it's okay as long as we get out of here before it hits.'

'You'll be lucky,' the driver offered unhelpfully. 'I've seen plenty of storms blowing in, and this will be a bad one.'

Jude sucked in a breath and swallowed hard. He could happily have strangled this cheerful harbinger of doom. Had the man no sense? What was the point in worrying them so when, in reality, they were still making good progress on the roads?

'So,' he said to Carrie in a deliberately buoyant tone. 'Do you reckon your mum has the turkey in the oven already?'

'Probably,' Carrie laughed. 'And dad will be on giblet duty. Or scrubbing potatoes. Or probably both.'

'I hope my parents go easy on the sherry.' Jude frowned as he imagined his dad holding forth on his unorthodox stance on politics and the state of the world economy. 'I didn't think about the fact that our parents might be together *without us* when I let Mr Whyte have my ticket yesterday.'

In honour of Maya's first Christmas, Jude and Carrie had agreed to have an all-family Christmas involving both sets of grandparents. After drawing lots, it had been decided that the event should take place at Carrie's parents' house. The two sets of grandparents had met several times before, of course – not always getting on famously – but they had unanimously decided that Christmas had to be celebrated together.

Being all too aware of the potential for familial catastrophe, Jude and Carrie had drawn up disaster avoidance plans on the many flights and bus journeys during The Blood Roses' US tour. None of these plans had involved leaving the opposing camps in a room together unsupervised.

'Gosh, I hope the turkey was a happy one,' Carrie laughed. 'Otherwise your mum will definitely *not* be happy.'

Jude's mum was a lapsed vegan and could justify eating meat only if it came from a farm with proven animal welfare credentials.

'"Was" being the operative word here,' Jude laughed. 'Because, of course, it won't be happy in the oven.'

'Stop it already, or I'm going vegetarian,' Carrie pouted, and Jude laughed some more. At least she had forgotten to worry about the snow.

But the worry returned, amplified manifold, when the cab pulled up in front of the airport. Even before they entered the terminal, Jude could see the chaos. Crowds of people were rushing this way or that with folks pushing against each other angrily. Long queues, piles of luggage, and arguing couples provided a stationary backdrop to the general mayhem.

'Good luck,' the driver wished them portentously as he unloaded their bags. 'I wouldn't leave it too long before you try to get back to the city, or you might be spending your Christmas right here.'

'Oh no, we won't,' Jude objected vehemently. 'It'll be fine.'

'Doubtful, my friend, doubtful. But you'll have to find out for yourselves.' With that, the driver jumped into his car and drove off. Jude smiled at Carrie, who was struggling to balance a once-more disgruntled Maya.

'We'll be fine,' he repeated. 'Let's go.'

Carrie smiled back weakly but said nothing. Doubt and fear were written all over her face, and Jude's heart constricted. He was anxious to get his little family checked in and through security; surely *then* Carrie would relax.

But checking in was proving difficult. As soon as they neared their airline desk, they were swallowed by a cloud of disorder. The queue for the London flight was hundreds of people deep. Hundreds of people who weren't moving.

It was impossible to make any sense of the cacophony of competing voices issuing information via the public address system, and Jude swivelled his eyes towards the departure boards. He was dismayed to read 'delayed' after 'delayed' after 'delayed' running down the far side of the screen. Not one flight had left JFK so far this morning.

Carrie had ambled off to grab a seat that had miraculously become vacant, and she jiggled Maya on her lap while Jude pondered the implications of their situation. Reluctantly, he spoke.

'I suppose this isn't looking great.'

'It's not, is it?' Carrie was eerily serene all of a sudden. 'It's not going to get better any time soon,' she remarked and nodded towards the glassy terminal walls. The outside world had all but disappeared in a cloud of white.

'Do you want me to try and get some sense out of the staff?' Jude offered doubtfully.

'No point. It'll be you and hundreds of other people. If they knew anything, we'd hear about it. You could try calling the airline's head office, maybe?'

'Good idea.'

Jude found the airline's local information number via Google but gave up after his tenth attempt of dialling. 'The switchboard is jammed.'

'Figures.' Carrie smiled weakly. Unexpectedly, her own mobile phone rang, and Jude took Maya while Carrie rooted around in her handbag to retrieve the device.

'Hello? Mum!' Carrie looked at Jude. 'It's Mum,' she mouthed.

'I gathered,' Jude whispered back.

'What's up?' Carrie returned her attention to the phone, and her face darkened. 'You what? — You're *sure?* — How do you know? — Yes…No, we're already at the airport. — Yes, it's pretty bad. — Oh yes, it's snowing. — Closed? What do you mean, closed?'

Carrie's voice rose on her last question. Jude looked at her anxiously, frustrated at not hearing the other part of the conversation.

'Okay. Yeah. Let me speak with Jude. I'll ring you back later. — Bye! — Love you too.'

She rang off and weighed the phone in her hands for a moment. Very deliberately, she put it back in her bag and claimed her daughter from Jude's arms.

'What did she say?' Jude couldn't keep the impatience and worry out of his voice.

'She said…' Carrie dropped her voice as though she was imparting state secrets. 'She says the news in England says that all of the East Coast airports have closed, and that no flights are expected to land or leave for the next twelve hours at least.'

'You what? Is she serious? Closed?'

'Keep your voice down,' Carrie hissed. 'If this gets out, there'll be a public transport nightmare. Let's cut our losses and grab a cab before there's a run on them.'

'Really? I mean, c'mon. She's all the way over there, and we're here. Look, the departure boards say nothing about flights being cancelled, just delayed.'

'Of course I'm sure. Why would she make it up?'

Jude shrugged. There was no reason why Carrie's mum would invent preposterous information such as this. She simply wasn't imaginative enough. But he refused to give up on their flight just yet.

'Suppose she's right,' he grumbled. 'Where would we go? Aren't we better off waiting it out?'

'I don't know. I don't fancy staying here.'

'Oh, Carrie. What a mess. But I still think we should hang on while there's a chance this might sort itself out. You know how sensation-lusty the British press is. I bet it's raining in the UK and they have nothing better to do than feast on someone else's snow.' He grinned, and Carrie was almost swayed.

'Look, I'll tell you what. Let's give it half an hour, and if the situation is unchanged, we'll go then. Okay?'

'Okay,' Carrie agreed.

'That's my girl.' Jude kissed his girlfriend on the cheek. 'As long as it merely says "delayed", I'm sure they'll — shit.'

'What?' Carrie was somewhat taken aback at Jude's abrupt swearword. Jude didn't answer at first but pulled her to her feet and grabbed the trolley with their cases at the same time.

'Let's go,' he instructed. 'Quick.'

'What's happened?'

Jude didn't reply, only subtly indicated the monitors overhead. Carrie followed his gaze and paled. The status of the first listed flight for the day had changed to cancelled. As Carrie watched, the other flights changed too, until the board was covered in red letters.

'Bollocks. Carrie, run. Grab a cab. Hurry.'

Jude struggled to turn around the trolley but pushed Carrie in the right direction. She gripped Maya tightly and strode out as quickly as she could. Other passengers had noticed the change in status, and there was general unrest.

Jude watched as Carrie flew out of the terminal and colonised one of the cabs waiting in line. He was finding it difficult to manoeuvre the luggage trolley through the crowds, but he pushed and shoved relentlessly. At the same time that he reached the exit, the public address system announced that the airport was now officially closed, and a groan rose from the disgruntled travellers. Jude lifted his suitcases and abandoned the trolley. He staggered the last few steps towards the cab that Carrie was holding for them. He threw the luggage into the boot and himself into the back seat. There were only three other cabs waiting, and already people were rushing to snag them.

'Hey buddy, what's the emergency?' the driver joked. 'Has the airport finally closed?'

'Certainly has,' Jude confirmed. 'Can you take us back to the city?' He gave the name of their hotel.

'Sure can,' the driver agreed. 'You'll probably be my last fare for the day. It might take a little while. The roads are awful. I was debating heading home anyway when your wife and daughter showed up in my backseat.'

'Is that so?' Jude replied distractedly.

'Sure is. I live in the city, so that's all good with me. You hold on tight now to your babe, ma'am. I don't have a child seat on board, but seeing as I'm a taxi, you can take her on your lap.'

'I know. It's okay,' Carrie assured. 'Doesn't look like you'll be going all that fast anyway.'

The driver, talkative though he was, had pulled away from the terminal whilst chatting, and they were beginning to make their way towards the interstate once more. Jude smiled at him but ignored the chatter. He took Carrie's hand and tickled Maya's nose.

'So, little princess, looks like you'll be spending your first Christmas in New York,' he murmured. Carrie burst into tears.

'I'm sorry,' Jude offered. 'If I hadn't swapped that ticket around, we'd be home safe and dry by now.'

'I know,' Carrie sniffed and tried to smile through her tears. 'But that's neither here nor there. It was an emergency, and you did the right thing. Only...'

She succumbed to a fresh wave of tears and her baby daughter, picking up on her mummy's distress, obligingly joined in with the crying. Jude felt out of his depth. The backseat was too narrow to hug either of his girls, and his soothing noises proved woefully inadequate to the task of calming down two distraught females.

He squeezed Carrie's hand hard and looked out of the window. The cab was crawling along at a snail's pace, and it was almost impossible to see the tail lights of the car in front. The world was literally white. Jude had never seen anything like it. His mind went round and round with questions and possibilities. What if they got stranded on the road? What if the cab had a crash?

'Jude?'

Carrie's voice cut through his thoughts, and he abandoned his worst-case scenarios.

'Jude, it's okay. I'm all right, really. It's just one of those things. I'm tired and hungry and a little overwhelmed. It's not the end of the world, though, right?'

'I hope not,' Jude responded, trying for levity. 'And at least we're together.'

'That's right. And hopefully, Mr Whyte watched his baby being born.'

'Yes. Let's hope he did,' Jude agreed dryly. 'Although we'll probably never find out.'

'No, I suppose not.' Carrie smiled again and gently bounced Maya up and down on her legs. The little girl had plugged her thumb in and calmed down.

'Jude, do you think the hotel will still have a room for us? I mean, it doesn't have to be the suite again, but a room would be good, right?'

'It's a big hotel. They're bound to have a room, however small.' Jude infused his voice with an optimism he didn't really feel.

'Could you… Maybe you could call ahead? And, you know, check?' Carrie suggested.

'Good idea, sweetpea. Why didn't I think of that?'

Jude searched through his pocket for the receipt he had been given at checkout—a receipt for zero dollars—and clicked open his mobile phone.

'Damn. No network. What about yours?'

Carrie clicked on her phone to check. 'Nothing.'

'We'll have to chance it,' Jude concluded. 'Man, but what a lot of snow.'

'Oh yeah,' the cab driver interjected from the front seat. 'And plenty more to come, I should think. It'll be a white Christmas for certain.'

'Great,' Carrie cheered unexpectedly. 'Just what I always wanted.'

'Really?' Jude was nonplussed.

'No.' Carrie grimaced. 'Only putting on a brave face.'

They stared at each other for a minute before erupting into laughter.

'We'll simply have to make the most of it,' Jude finally gasped.

'Yeah, as you said earlier… we'll talk about this for years to come. "Remember the Christmas we got stuck in New York?"'

'And we stayed in the poshest hotel known to man?' Jude picked up her thread.

'And we had Christmas dinner in our five-star suite in front of the fire?'

'With mulled cider?'

'And champagne!'

'No washing up!'

'No arguing rellies!'

'This could be quite good, actually,' Carrie summed up. 'As long as we can let our parents know that we're safe, of course.' She tapped on her mobile phone. 'Still no signal.'

'We'll use the landline in the hotel,' Jude promised, 'as soon as we've checked in.'

They fell silent after that, letting the rest of the long journey wash over them. The cab driver sang Christmas tunes under his breath until they finally pulled up in front of the hotel, by which time it was past three o'clock.

Jude, Carrie, and Maya piled out of the cab, and Jude led the way into the hotel. They had to scramble over large drifts of snow as the porter had evidently given up the fight against the heavily falling flakes. The road was completely invisible, and Park Avenue was more or less unrecognisable.

'If it weren't such an inconvenience, I'd say it's very pretty,' Carrie said. 'God, I can't wait to get warm and maybe have a bath. Plus Maya could do with a new nappy.'

'Not long now,' Jude soothed. 'Let's see what we can get.'

They stumbled into the lobby that they had left a seeming lifetime ago and entered an oasis of light, warmth, and calm. Jude brushed the snowflakes off his coat and surrendered the suitcases once again to a bellhop. Carrie whispered that she had better take care of Maya before there was a major leakage and ambled off towards the ladies' room. Jude, meanwhile, strode purposefully to the reception desk and greeted the receptionist like a long-lost friend.

'I gather you didn't make your flight, sir?' the receptionist enquired solicitously.

'We most certainly didn't,' Jude confirmed. 'The airport is closed until this storm is over.'

'So I hear,' the receptionist agreed. 'And what can I do for you?'

Jude looked at him blankly and bit back a tart response. A feeling of dread took hold of his heart like an iron clamp, and he swallowed hard. He would have thought that it was obvious what they wanted. Nonetheless, he smiled and opened his mouth to ask as politely as he could.

'A room for the night, perhaps? That would be good.'

He had aimed for mild irony, but the receptionist's face fell.

'I was worried you'd say that.'

'You were?'

'I was. You see… We're full. Completely booked. No room left.'

'No room left?' Jude echoed, incredulous. 'Not a one?'

'No room left.'

'What's up?' Carrie asked innocently, having missed the exchange up to now. Jude turned to her, his smile frozen on his face.

'There's no room at the inn.'

'What?'

'No room at the inn,' Jude quipped. 'It appears we're to be like Mary and Joseph. Except, of course, you're not pregnant. That's something at least.'

~ 3 ~

In the Bleak Midwinter

'And you're absolutely sure there's nothing you can do for us? Not even a broom closet?' Jude pleaded with the receptionist. 'We'll take anything. A staff room. Anything.'

The receptionist shook his head for the sixteenth time. 'I'm so sorry sir, but we're full. All the duty staff are staying over, and they're doubling up on rooms as it is. It's pretty much the same in hotels all over the city, or so I hear. I'm so sorry.'

'But what will you have us do?' Carrie sounded distraught. 'We have a baby and all...'

'I know that, ma'am. Believe me, if I could help...' The receptionist trailed off.

'Now what?' Carrie turned to Jude. 'Now what?'

Jude chewed his bottom lip. This whole situation was becoming a nightmare, albeit a very real one.

'Can we at least leave our suitcases in your luggage room for a little while? I'm sure Mr Whyte will appreciate hearing how well you helped his erstwhile *guests* in their hour of need.'

Jude had no idea how this idea had jumped into his head, but the receptionist paled at the mention of Mr Whyte's name.

'Of course,' he agreed hastily. 'If that would help sir and ma'am, then of course you can stow your luggage with us for a short time.'

Encouraged by this small victory, Jude pressed on. 'Is your restaurant open? May we at least get a meal?'

'Why, of course.' The receptionist hesitated only for a heartbeat. 'You're not technically guests, but would you like a table for three?'

'Yes, please. Right away, if you can. We're starving.' Jude summoned a smile and turned to Carrie. 'C'mon, sweetheart, let's get some food. We'll feel better then.'

He led Carrie and Maya towards the less formal dining room. The lunch rush was over, and it was too early for evening diners, so the place was only moderately busy. Jude and Carrie gratefully sat down at a table. Carrie ordered steak and fries for herself and the soup for Maya, and Jude had a burger. The food was hot and fragrant and lifted their spirits no end.

'And now?' Carrie challenged when she had finished her last bite of steak. 'We're warm and fed, but where do we go from here?'

Jude shrugged and scooped another teaspoonful of soup into Maya's mouth. The little girl kicked her legs in delight. It appeared that the upmarket soup tickled her tiny taste buds.

'I don't know,' he finally acknowledged. 'I think we should hang around and hope something turns up. I can't see them throwing us out for the night, can you?'

Carrie shook her head. 'I'm not sure this is such a good idea. They'll get us arrested for loitering or something.'

Jude grinned. 'That's not a bad idea. I bet it'll be warm and dry in prison, and we might even get a free meal.'

His smile faded when he saw Carrie's face fall. Tears were shimmering in her eyes, and he wrapped his arm around her shoulder to try and comfort her.

'It's Christmas Eve,' she whispered. 'I don't want to spend Christmas Eve in a hotel lobby or, God forbid –', she hiccupped in horror, ' – in a prison cell. That's not how I imagined Maya's first Christmas!'

'I know,' Jude soothed her. 'I know. I was only kidding. We'll work something out. I know we will.'

'But what? You heard the man. Everywhere is booked up. How are we going to work something out?'

Jude shrugged. 'Honestly, sweetie, at this point I haven't got a clue. But I can't see us being on the streets for Christmas Eve. Something will turn up. I have faith.'

He spoke with utter conviction and discovered, to his great surprise, that he actually believed his own words. He had no idea what was going to happen, but he knew they were going to be fine.

'How can you say that? How can you be so sure?' Carrie dissolved in more tears, and Jude's heart nearly broke.

'I don't know. But it's *Christmas*. Magical things happen at Christmas.'

'We don't need magic. We need a bloody miracle.'

'Language, language,' Jude chided her affectionately. 'Little ears are listening in.' He chuckled and rose. 'If it's a miracle you're after, we'd better go in search of one. C'mon, let's take a walk.'

'A walk?' Carrie's eyes opened wide with incredulity. 'In this weather? Are you nuts?'

'Only a little. *Walk*, I mean. I'm quite sane. Trust me.'

Carrie shook her head once more but stood up anyway, lifting Maya out of her high chair as she did. 'I suppose you're right. Why not indeed? At least it's something to do, right?'

'Right,' Jude grinned. 'Let's tog up and take a look at New York in the snow.'

They stood outside the hotel for a moment, trying to get their bearings. Snow continued to fall heavily, and the traffic on Park Avenue was at a near standstill. All sounds were muffled by the adverse weather, and the city that supposedly never slept was eerily quiet.

'We must be mad,' Carrie reiterated.

'Not at all,' Jude contradicted. 'I think it's romantic. A walk in the snow in the Big Apple on Christmas Eve. This is definitely one for the books!'

Carrie laughed and nudged him gently, thick winter coat against thick winter coat. Her face was barely visible. She had wrapped a woolly scarf around her mouth and nose so that only her eyes peered out from under her big hat. Jude looked similar, with the addition of a heavily wrapped and be-hatted Maya in the sling on his chest.

'You look like a yeti,' Carrie remarked.

Jude placed his arms protectively around his daughter and bounced up and down on the balls of his feet. 'This yeti carries precious cargo. Now, which way shall we go?'

Carrie turned to face left and then right, but both directions looked equally bleak. 'I think Central Park is that way,' she pointed. 'It's as good a destination as any.'

'Let's go,' Jude agreed. He took one of her gloved hands in his, and together they trudged out into the snowy cityscape.

They walked in silence for a while, focusing on finding a rhythm for their feet in the sticky white snow, occasionally sliding on patches of ice. Jude's heart lifted with every step. While this wasn't what he had planned for his little family, it was a definite adventure, and he could never resist the little-boy excitement that blossomed inside him at severe weather. He knew Carrie was worried, but he hoped that she too would enjoy this most unusual experience. He gripped her gloved hand more firmly and felt her fingers squeeze his in response.

Apart from Jude and Carrie, there were few pedestrians about. Compared to the previous day, the streets were deserted. It seemed that New Yorkers had holed up in their homes, taking shelter from the inclement weather.

'Gives a whole new meaning to the old saying, "Only mad dogs and Englishmen…",' Jude shouted.

'Yeah,' Carrie agreed. 'I always thought it was more apt to talk about dogs and *mad* Englishmen anyway…'

'Hey,' Jude suddenly laughed. He swivelled his free hand about as though twirling a walking stick. Then he stuck his chest out, baby girl strapped to his front notwithstanding, thrust his head back, and swaggered on for a few paces. 'Who am I?'

Carrie stood and observed. 'I've no idea.'

'Here's another clue.' Jude pretended to lift a cup to his mouth and pulled a face. 'I don't drink coffee…'

'I get it! You drink tea! You're an Englishman who's very definitely in New York!'

'Well done!' Jude allowed Carrie to catch up with him and gave her a hearty pat on the shoulder. 'Your turn.'

'Me? What, now? Here? You want me to play charades?'

'Why not? It's a Christmas Eve tradition!'

'Yeah, but normally it involves a roaring fire, a large circle of friends, and some mulled wine.'

'True,' Jude conceded. 'I'll have to work on those. But hey… Listen up. What's this?'

He cocked an ear to the extent that that was possible under his woollen hat.

'Carol singers,' Carrie exclaimed. She turned through three hundred and sixty degrees on the spot, trying to locate the source of the faint singing. 'I think they're this way.'

She strode out further along Park Avenue. Jude followed her until they reached the intersection with East 53rd Street. There, on the corner, stood a small cluster of men bravely singing their hearts out despite the freezing cold and ongoing white-out.

'Oh my God. Please tell me they're not singing "Galway Bay",' Carrie said.

'They're not. And they're not the boys from the NYPD choir either,' Jude observed laughingly.

'They're not? How do you know?'

'Because there is no NYPD choir.'

'There isn't?' Carrie's eyes flashed with disappointment. 'Really?'

'Nope, they made it up. The Pogues did, I mean.'

'Gosh, this *is* a night for shattering illusions,' Carrie chortled. 'Wouldn't it have been awesome if we'd come across the *real* NYPD choir?'

'Yeah. That would have been quite "Fairytale of New York",' Jude agreed. He looped his arm around Carrie and drew her close while they both tried to make out the song. Fragments of lyrics drifted their way.

Snow was falling, snow on snow...

'...in the bleak midwinter, long, long ago,' Carrie joined in hoarsely. 'What an appropriate song.'

'I'm surprised they know it,' Jude mused. 'It's very British, and even at home it's hardly mainstream.'

The song finished, and the singers stood at ease. Carrie applauded wildly, but her gloved hands made only a muffled sound. She stepped forward until the small choir caught sight of her, and then she clapped some more. The men smiled and took a bow.

'Glad you liked it, miss,' one of them shouted.

'I loved it,' Carrie shouted back. 'Are you going to do any more songs?'

'Ah no, we're packing up,' the singer responded, leaving the group and taking a few steps towards Carrie.

'We've been here two hours, and it's real cold. There's no one around. We're gonna call it a day.'

Jude stepped up and pressed a couple of folded bills into the collection tin the man was holding. 'Merry Christmas,' he offered.

'Thanks a lot, sir. We're collecting for the children's hospital, and your donation will be appreciated.'

Jude inclined his head, and Carrie spoke up again.

'I loved that song you sang. You know, "In the bleak midwinter". It's one of my favourites and…'

A fat tear escaped her eye, and she swiped at it quickly. 'Sorry. I'm a bit upset. Sorry.'

The singer looked from Carrie to Jude and back again. 'Are you okay?'

Jude put his arm around Carrie once more and answered on her behalf. 'We're a little stuck. There's no room at the inn for us tonight.'

'Sorry, what?' Befuddlement was written on the singer's face.

'We were supposed to go back to London this morning, but the airport closed, and now we're stranded,' Jude explained. 'The hotel is full, and we literally have no place to stay. That's why my girlfriend is so upset. Hearing that song made her even more homesick, I think.'

'Ah. I see.' The singer rubbed his chin.

'How do you know the song anyway? It's not really a traditional carol over here. Or is it?'

'Nah. James taught it to us. He's from Peterborough.' He pronounced the name of the unfamiliar English town as 'Pete-barah', and Jude suppressed a smile. 'James thought the tourists would like it.'

'Well, we certainly did,' Jude agreed. 'Peterborough, wow. That's a long way to come. Is he here? It would be nice to say hello.'

The singer shifted uncomfortably on his feet. 'He's not. He went home for Christmas three days ago.'

'Ah. Good for him.' Jude hugged Carrie a little closer still. 'Have a lovely Christmas now.' He turned to walk away, pulling Carrie with him, but the singer stopped them.

'Wait, wait. Are you saying you really have nowhere to stay?'

'Yup, that's about the size of it.'

'What, with the little one, too?'

'Uh-huh.'

'Hmmm…' The singer rubbed his chin with his gloved hand. He peered at Jude and Carrie intently. 'Hey… Didn't I see you in the little Italian place downtown yesterday? With the babe asleep on the seat?'

'Um… Yeah, that's possible,' Jude agreed cautiously. 'We did have lunch…'

'I knew it.' The singer gave a big air-punch. 'I love your voices. You know, your British accent.' He put on a plummy voice as he continued speaking. '"How do you do" and all that… "Ray," I said to myself, "Ray, these folks are from the other side of the pond."'

He grinned at them both widely, holding his arms out as though he was planning to hug them. 'I knew I'd seen you before. Ha! Let me see what I can come up with. Can't have a nice Briddish family like you guys stranded here all by their lonesomes on Christmas Eve.'

Carrie looked at the singer, a sudden hope gleaming in her eyes. 'Can you... Do you know of... Do you think you might be able to help us?'

'I just might,' the singer agreed exuberantly. 'Not personally, of course, because our little apartment is rammed as it is, what with the kids and everything... But my brother, he runs a small hotel. It's more of a hostel, really, very basic, nothing fancy, but it would be warm and dry at least. *If* it's available.'

'Oh, please, could you check?' Carrie pleaded. 'I wouldn't normally jump on an offer like this, especially as we don't even know each other, but I'm tired and hungry and scared, and I hadn't planned for our daughter to be homeless on her first Christmas... Please?'

'Of course I'll check.' He extended a hand. 'I'm Ray.'

'Carrie.' Carrie shook his hand. 'And this is Jude.'

Jude and Ray nodded at each other.

'There, now. Now we know each other, and you don't need to feel awkward no more,' Ray chuckled.

Jude warmed to the fellow by the minute. Whether he was a genuinely nice man or whether he was trying to rip them off—he didn't know, and he didn't care, as long as it put a roof over their heads for the night.

'Thanks,' he addressed Ray. 'It would mean the world.'

'Lemme make a call,' Ray suggested. 'See if Louis is in.'

He dug a mobile phone out of his coat pocket and punched in a few numbers. Carrie and Jude shuffled away to give him some privacy, even though Jude was desperate to eavesdrop and hear how the conversation was going.

The other members of the choir were saying their farewells, shaking hands and clapping each other's backs, and it was obvious that Jude and Carrie were holding Ray up.

'Oh God, this is really awkward,' Carrie muttered. 'If we weren't so desperate…'

'Desperate no more,' Ray interrupted, slapping Jude on the back. 'Sorry, didn't mean to listen in but couldn't help hearing what you said. You're in luck. One of Louis's apartments is free. Not much call for your basic accommodation over Christmas, it appears. He would be delighted to let it to you for the night, or for however long you need.'

'Really?' Carrie squealed and jumped up and down with glee.

'Hopefully one or two nights will see us right,' Jude said at the same time, feeling a little less able to express his joy in quite as exultant a manner as Carrie. 'That would be tremendous, thank you.'

'Now,' Ray gushed, 'let me say goodbye to the boys, and I'll take you right over there…'

'Oh no, you don't have to do that, we can take a cab,' Jude objected hastily. The last thing he wanted was to put Ray out any more than was strictly necessary.

'You won't find a taxi for love or money now, and besides, I'm going over there anyway, so I might as well take you. Always assuming you haven't left your luggage somewhere downtown. You do have luggage, right?'

'We do. And it's only a couple of blocks that way,' Carrie clarified.

'Oh good. Hang on.' Ray loped off, skidding on a patch of black ice, and exchanged a few quick words with his choir. He was back in an instant.

'Ready? The apartment is in a small hostel on East 104th Street. It's really quite safe there, and you'll be comfortable at least. It's only forty bucks a night, I hope that's all right.'

'Forty bucks?' Jude mouthed at Carrie. He had visions of mouldy ceilings, broken windows, and dark stairwells.

'Yup. Toldya it's cheap, but it's clean and warm. The Waldorf it ain't, but you'll be off the streets. Now, where are your things?'

'Um. At a hotel. Down that way.' Jude cringed at how this would look to Ray and quickly launched into the story of how they came to stay in a five-star luxury hotel.

'No kiddin' me?' Ray bellowed. 'He gave you his suite, just like that?'

'Well, he had paid for it and wasn't using it any longer…'

Ray chuckled. 'You know what they say, right? Anything can happen in the Big Apple, and you're living proof. What a story. Can't wait to tell this to my Bella. Bella's my wife, by the way.'

Jude nodded but didn't know how else to respond. Ray had set a brisk pace in the direction of the hotel. It was as if he didn't even notice the snow and ice, and Jude and Carrie struggled to keep up. Quite unexpectedly, he stopped.

'Here's my ride. Hop in. I'll drive you round there and on to Louis's place.'

He unlocked the police cruiser and held open the rear door.

Carrie looked at Jude. Jude looked at Carrie. Ray looked at them both.

'What?' he asked. 'This is my car. I'm off duty. You can take a ride, hop on in.'

'You're a police officer?' Carrie verified.

'At your service, ma'am,' Ray replied and gave a jokey salute. 'Although off duty, as previously stated. And this old thing...' He gave the car an affectionate pat. 'Her name is Matilda. She was the real deal, but she's second hand. I bought her at auction for my personal use.'

'Wow. So *nearly* the NYPD choir after all, and a retired cruiser by the name Matilda to top it all off,' Carrie chortled and got a blank stare from Ray.

'Long story,' Jude intervened. 'Don't mind her. She's happy to have found some help. Thank you, Ray, really. It's awesome to think that in this day and age, strangers still help strangers.'

Ray shrugged. 'It's nothing. And it's Christmas. Plus it's what anyone would do, right?'

An hour later, Ray deposited them outside an apartment building in East Harlem after a slow and anxious drive through the ongoing blizzard. Despite the circumstances, Carrie had marvelled at the setting all the way through the journey.

'Look at these houses, and the trees, and the wide roads… It's like the set of Friends,' she had exclaimed. 'I feel like I know this place.'

'Not quite,' Ray had dampened her enthusiasm. 'That building is in Greenwich Village, but I do know what you mean. If you haven't been to New York before, a lot of places probably feel very familiar from the many TV shows you've seen.'

Carrie had barely paid him any attention. Jude smiled to himself. Yesterday's official sightseeing tour had fascinated her plenty, but seeing the 'real' New York seemed to capture her imagination even more. Perhaps this stay would be a good thing, a good memory for them in years to come.

Jude momentarily lost himself in reflection, sensing the outline of a song at the edge of his mind. But he snapped back to the present moment when Ray retrieved the keys to their temporary abode from a letterbox on the ground floor.

'Here you go,' Ray declared.

'Thanks so much.' Jude proffered four ten-dollar bills for Ray to pass on to his brother.

'I'm seeing him now, actually,' Ray grinned. 'Round the corner from here. It's our Christmas Eve family meal. *La Vigilia di Natale.*' He beamed at Jude and Carrie's uncomprehending faces. 'We may be third-generation Italian immigrants, but we still honour some of our native traditions. Today, it's a big dinner, followed by church and a first present for the little ones. We kinda merge all sorts of cultures.'

'Ah,' Jude replied. Carrie looked stricken once more at the mention of 'family traditions'. No doubt she was thinking about all the family stuff that Jude, Carrie, and Maya *wouldn't* be doing that evening.

Ray, too, picked up on the change of mood. He smiled wistfully and shrugged at the same time. 'I'm sorry you're on your own here, folks, that must be tough. Anyway...' He shrugged some more. 'I must be off. There's a bodega round the corner where you should be able to get some food for tonight.' He gestured towards the end of the road. Jude and Carrie obligingly looked that way, but the turning was invisible through the heavy snow fall.

'Yeah, well, it's along there, and then hang a left. You can't miss it.' Ray shuffled on his feet. It seemed he was embarrassed at having to leave them to their own devices. Jude summoned a smile and jingled the apartment keys in his hand.

'Thanks, Ray. We'll be fine. Have a good evening, now, and merry Christmas to you and your family.'

'Merry Christmas,' Ray responded. He threw them a last apologetic glance before climbing back into his car and driving very slowly down the road.

'Well, up we go,' Jude declared staunchly. 'Let's see what this place has to offer. You take Maya, I'll take the luggage.'

Up they lumbered, one flight of stairs, and another, and finally a third. Apartment thirty-six was at the end of a long, narrow corridor that almost, but not quite, lived up to Jude's expectations of a dark and miserable dive. He set the suitcases down and unlocked the door with some trepidation. Perhaps they had been foolish to accept the stranger's offer of abode. Perhaps they would have been wiser to throw themselves on the mercy of the hotel. Still, too late now.

He stepped into the apartment gingerly and cast an anxious look around while he took off his hat and scarf. There was one large room featuring a double bed, sofa, small table, television and wardrobe. To the right, there a kitchenette and a door that presumably led to the bathroom. The décor was dated but neutral, and the place smelled fresh. There was no evidence of mould, damp, or insect infestation.

Carrie squeezed past him and rushed to the bed. She lifted the covers up hesitantly and, after a quick look, buried her nose in the fabric.

'Oh thank God, it's clean,' she declared.

Jude breathed a silent sigh of relief. 'It ain't the Ritz, but it beats a stable,' he picked up on his earlier joke.

'It certainly does,' Carrie agreed. She put Maya on the big bed and took off her own and her daughter's coats, hanging them on the back of a chair. Jude noted that a certain sparkle had returned to her eyes. Evidently she had accepted the inevitable and was rallying fast. His heart swelled with love for this amazing woman.

Carrie moved around the room, feeling the radiator and prattling on. 'It's warm. And I presume there is running water. I could do with a nice, hot shower. I feel frozen to the core. As for munchkin here…' She bent over and kissed her daughter's downy head. Maya gurgled and kicked her legs. 'She would probably enjoy a little splash, and she should really have a nap. What's the time, anyway?'

'It's five o'clock.'

'Blimey.' Carrie yawned. 'No wonder I'm knackered. Oh, for a nice cup of tea.'

'Hey, listen...' Jude wrapped his girlfriend in his arms. 'How's about you ladies get freshened up and rested, and I venture out to see if I can't get some basic provisions from this bodega Ray mentioned?'

'Ooooh...' Carrie's eyes went round with joy. 'Would you do that? Aren't you cold and tired?'

'Yes, to both,' Jude laughed, 'but I can still pull off the hunter-gatherer act for my girls. Besides, I'd kill for a cuppa, so needs must.'

Carrie smiled and gave Jude a fat kiss on the lips. 'I love you, rock star.'

'I love you, too, honeykins.'

'Don't get lost in the snow, will you?'

'Of course not.' Jude grinned and zipped up his coat once more. He wound his scarf round his neck and face and put on his hat. His voice emerged muffled but cheerful. 'I'll be back in a tick with the most amazing Christmas feast.'

~ 4 ~

Ring Out Solstice Bells

'So we've got…'

Jude gave a little drumroll on the table as he prepared to unpack his shopping. Carrie and Maya had emerged from the shower, warm and damp and pink and wrapped in blankets over their pyjamas. Carrie laid Maya down for a snooze on the big bed. Jude rummaged around in his shopping bag and set item by item of his loot on the table.

'Tea. Sugar. Milk. Wine. Bread. Tinned ham…'

'Tinned ham?' Carrie interrupted. 'Let's see. Is that the same stuff they fight over in *Christmas with the Kranks*?'

'No idea. If it's hickory honey ham they're after, then yes.'

Carrie chuckled. 'Yay. I always wondered what that was about. Now we can find out.'

'Indeed,' Jude smiled matter-of-factly and continued unpacking. 'Olives. Jam. Crackers. Potato *chips*.' He placed a comic emphasis on the word 'chips' which, to him, signified fat chunks of deep-fried potato known to Americans as 'fries.'

'Cranberry sauce. Apples. Chocolate. Cheese. Oh, and a yummy-looking can of chicken broth for Maya.'

'Wow. What a spread!'

'Apologies for the lack of turkey. They were clean out.' Jude pulled a funny face.

'Seriously?'

'Nah. They didn't stock turkey. Too small a shop.'

Carrie shrugged. 'Never mind. I don't like turkey anyway.'

Jude gasped. 'Really? You don't like turkey?'

Carrie shook her head. 'Nope.'

'Well, you kept that quiet over the past few years. Now the truth comes out.'

'I know.' Carrie laughed. 'And while I'm at it, I might as well confess that I hate sprouts. *And* parsnips.'

Jude exploded with laughter. 'So really, you don't like Christmas dinner at all?'

'Nope. This—' Carrie indicated the erratic spread of food on the table, 'to me is as good as any.' She rose and rearranged their goodies. 'Tonight we shall dine festively on ham with roast potatoes, roast apples, and cranberry sauce, with a starter of toasted bread with olives and a pudding of…' She lifted a packet and eyed it dubiously. 'Extra special luxury chocolate. Perfect.'

'I suppose that's *nearly* a Christmas dinner,' Jude chortled. 'All the right ingredients, mostly.'

'Yeah. Let's get cooking. What do we do with this thing?' Carrie stood the tinned ham on its side and rolled it across the table. 'Does it need heating up, or do you eat it cold?'

'No idea,' Jude confessed. 'What does it say on the tin?'

'It doesn't,' Carrie replied. 'I think you're supposed to know.'

'Ah. Hm.'

Jude and Carrie stood quietly while they contemplated what to do with their ham.

Gently, almost imperceptibly, an unexpected sound permeated their silence. Jude heard it first. He frowned and looked around in surprise. Carrie caught his eyes.

'Do you hear them?' she whispered. 'Church bells.'

'I do,' Jude whispered back. 'Although I thought I was imagining it.'

Carrie crossed the room to the small window and peered out into the darkness.

'It's still snowing like there's no tomorrow,' she commented. 'I can't see a thing. But there are definitely bells. Quite close too, otherwise we wouldn't hear them.'

'It must be the Christmas Eve service,' Jude surmised.

'Of course.' Carrie pressed her forehead against the cool glass of the window. 'You're right.'

Jude picked up the tin of ham again and turned it over in his hands, looking once more for eating—or heating—instructions. He didn't give the bells another thought until Carrie spoke into his ear.

'Shall we go?'

'What? Go where?'

'To church.' Carrie's voice was soft, her breath warm against his skin. He turned to face her.

'You want to go to church?'

Carrie nodded.

'Why?' Jude was completely surprised by her suggestion. 'I mean… We've never been to church together. Like, ever. Not even at Christmas. I didn't know that this was your thing.'

Carrie laughed. 'It isn't "my thing." But… I don't know. It seems a good thing to do, somehow. Don't ask me why. It's not like we have anything else to do, right?'

Jude didn't respond for a moment but listened out for the bells that continued ringing. He gave an inward shrug.

'Okay,' he agreed amiably. 'Why not? Maybe I'll have some sort of epiphany about this ham while we're out.' For some reason, he felt compelled to crack a feeble joke, but Carrie didn't comment on it.

'Oh lovely,' she breathed. 'Let's go. It can't be far.'

So they got dressed in their winter coats and accessories all over again.

Wrapped like polar explorers, they ventured forth once more into the unrelenting storm, Jude carrying Maya in her sling as before. The sidewalks were piled high with snowdrifts. The night was bright with flurries of thick white flakes, and the effect was one of a strange half-light. Maya babbled and chuckled in glee, reaching out her tiny gloves to touch some of the flakes.

Carrie laughed. 'If she had more coordination already, she'd be eating snowflakes right now. She's fascinated by the stuff.'

'Her and me both,' Jude agreed. 'I've never seen anything like this. It hasn't stopped since six a.m. this morning. It's like *The Day After Tomorrow*.'

'Gosh, I hope not. That would be *really* cold.' She gave an exaggerated shiver, than held up a hand. 'Now, where are those bells coming from? It's hard to tell.'

'This way,' Jude suggested. 'Let's take a look.'

They took a few hesitant steps into the direction he indicated and, sure enough, the tolling of bells became louder. Encouraged, they strode out a little faster, and they soon found the church.

'It's right here,' Carrie exclaimed and skidded to a halt.

The building didn't look very church-like from the outside. It was seamlessly integrated into the frontage of the surrounding buildings, and if it hadn't been for the tall arched stained-glass windows lit up from within, they might have walked right past it. But now that they had stopped, they noted an entrance. The door was closed, presumably to keep out the snow and the cold, but a sign invited them to step inside.

Our Christmas Eve Service is open to all, the note read. *Come and join us.*

'Go on,' Jude encouraged Carrie. 'Let's do it. You go in first.'

'Are you shy all of a sudden, Mr Big Important Rock Star?' Carrie teased.

'Not at all. But I haven't got a clue what the protocol is in there.'

'Well.' Carrie nudged his shoulder and brushed some snow off his hat. 'I suppose we go in and sit down and see what happens.'

'All righty.'

Jude pulled open the door for Carrie and let her step in. He followed her and made sure the door was properly closed before examining their surroundings.

Wooden pews stood in two long rows perpendicular to the length of the building. To the far right was the nave with the altar. A red carpet ran from the entrance to the centre aisle and all the way to the front. A large Christmas tree adorned the back. The room was lit entirely with candles, giving it a festive, warm atmosphere.

An organ played quietly, and there was a low hum of voices from the small congregation. Jude felt a little awkward, like an intruder, but Carrie blithely found a seat in the back pew and settled herself down. She patted the space next to her and smiled at Jude. He walked across and unclipped Maya from her harness. The little girl looked around with wide eyes, mesmerised by the many flickering candles. Jude sat down, cradling his daughter on his lap, and whispered to Carrie.

'And now?'

'Now we go with the flow,' Carrie replied. 'I've no idea what happens next. But isn't it beautiful? And festive?' Her eyes gleamed, and Jude smiled. It certainly was beautiful and festive. He sat back and tried to relax. Soon, the atmosphere worked its magic on him, and he was overcome all Christmassy. He found himself smiling and unable to stop.

Within moments, the sound of the organ swelled as the unseen organist launched into the first hymn. The congregation stood, and so did Jude and Carrie. Dressed in robes and other churchly garments, the priest and choir processed up the aisle in time to the carol. The voices of the singers rose powerfully above the organ, and Jude shivered.

'This is great,' he said under his breath, but Carrie heard him anyway.

'I know. It's like proper Christmas all of a sudden.'

For the next forty-five minutes, Jude and Carrie listened to the story of the birth of Jesus and sang Christmas hymns. Against every expectation, Jude was completely swept away by the atmosphere. He couldn't work out why; perhaps it was the magic of rites remembered from his childhood, or the bliss of lifting his voice to join in with the carols, or simply the ancient warmth of dozens of candles.

He took hold of Carrie's hand and squeezed it tight. A quick glance at the two most important ladies in his life told him that even baby Maya was consumed by the service, if only in the sense that it had lulled her to sleep. He was almost disappointed when the service came to an end.

'That was lovely,' Carrie beamed as the final note of the last carol faded and the members of the congregation started rising and chatting to each other. 'Thank you. I feel very Christmassy.'

'I enjoyed it, too,' Jude agreed. 'I didn't really know what to expect, but I feel weirdly uplifted.'

'I think that's the general idea,' Carrie laughed.

'Just don't go all holy on me now,' Jude cautioned, half joking and half serious. 'I'm not sure I'm ready for that.'

'I won't. Although perhaps we could do this again sometime, you know. Maybe next Christmas, at home. It's a start, right?'

A start to what? Jude longed to ask, but never he got the chance.

'Jude! Carrie! And Maya, too! Hey, you guys. Merry Christmas!'

'Ray!' Carrie was the first to recover from the surprise greeting. 'Wow. Hey. Fancy meeting you here. Merry Christmas to you, again!' She smiled widely.

'Merry Christmas, Ray,' Jude echoed automatically. 'How extraordinary, seeing you again.'

'Not at all, not at all,' Ray grinned. 'This is my parish church after all. My brother Louis lives round the corner. I never thought to mention the church when I dropped you off, but I'm glad you found it. Hey, is the apartment okay?'

'It's wonderful,' Carrie gushed.

Ray chortled. 'Well, I wouldn't go quite that far, but hopefully it's clean and warm, as promised.'

'It is. *And* there's plenty of hot water,' Carrie replied.

Ray looked a little taken aback, so Jude offered an explanation. 'Give her a hot shower anywhere, and she'll feel right at home.'

'Ah, yes. My wife's the same,' Ray agreed. 'Come, come, meet my family.'

He gestured broadly towards the front of the church, and Jude obediently began walking in that direction. Carrie followed with Maya.

There was much exclaiming and shouting when Ray introduced his three British 'foundlings' to his assembled family. The ensuing chatter of voices sent Jude's head spinning, and he didn't know who to respond to first.

'Do you like the apartment?' — That had to be Louis.

'Have you eaten? What are you doing for Christmas dinner?' — A large female with grey hair and a vividly coloured scarf. A grandmother?

'How old is the baby?' — A slender female with luscious black hair.

'How did you like our service?' — One of the choristers.

'Ah, guys, slow down, slow down!' Ray erupted into a barrage of Italian that Jude didn't understand. His hands spoke as quickly as his mouth, and the effect was noisy and powerful. Everybody quietened down, and all eyes were on Carrie and Jude.

'Um,' Carrie uttered, nonplussed. 'The apartment is fine, thank you. Maya is six months old. And we have organised a little meal for ourselves for Christmas. Jude found the bodega…'

'The *bodega*?' Grandmother-figure shrieked in horror.

'The bodega?' The younger female snorted dismissively. 'That's junk you get in there. You need proper food.'

'Ah, the bodega, you found it,' Ray muttered weakly.

More Italian chatter followed this revelation, hands going every which way, up, down, and round and round. Carrie and Jude exchanged a silent glance. Jude saw that Carrie was biting her lips as if suppressing a laugh, and he looked away quickly before he would burst out laughing himself. He had a strong feeling that a plan was being hatched on their behalf, a plan involving food and family, and he was trying to work out how to respond. He wouldn't feel comfortable imposing on these perfect strangers, however well-intentioned they turned out to be.

In the event, he didn't have to respond. After an energetic shooing gesture by Ray, his family waved at Carrie and Jude and moved down the aisle in one big gaggle of ongoing banter.

'Phew,' Ray exhaled sharply. 'Sorry about that. The women can get a bit overexcited. They like to entertain, and any new victim is always welcome.' He grinned. 'They're off to get all the food ready. *We* have something else to do.'

'We?' Jude pounced immediately.

'*All* the food?' Carrie was focused on something else. 'I thought you said you'd have dinner before church?'

'That's what I thought, but there wasn't enough time. And now I have another call of duty. Would you like to join me?'

'Join you in what?' Jude was confused.

'Ah. Well. I'm on Santa duty tonight at the children's hospital. I go over there and deliver presents, and we have a little sing along. It won't take long, but they do like it so. The children, I mean. Not all of them have family that can visit over the holidays. What with all this snow, I suppose there will be quite a few lonely little ones there tonight, and…' He shrugged. 'It's something I do every year, snow or not.'

'Oh wow,' Carrie cried. 'That sounds… That sounds amazing.'

Jude swallowed. It did sound amazing, but it also sounded a little odd. He wasn't used to this level of caring and charity, and it wouldn't have occurred to him to do anything like this on his own. His gut instinct was to decline, but his heart said, *go on, do it.*

~ 5 ~

Do They Know It's Christmas?

'...and then the Grinch joined in with the party and everybody had a wonderful time.'

Jude listened from the corridor as Carrie summed up the story. She was entertaining the children in the dayroom. One of the nurses had introduced her to the kids and equipped her with a story book to read while Jude and Ray had gone off to organise Santa. Jude presumed that Maya was in there with her as well, although she was very quiet.

'I don't like the Grinch,' a little boy remarked.

'Why don't you like him, Luke?' came Carrie's response. Jude could hear the emotion in her voice.

'I don't trust him. Once evil, always evil.'

'*I* like him,' a little girl piped up. 'I think he's a softie, really.'

'I don't like green people,' another girl observed. 'If you're green, you're sick, and that's sad.'

There was a silence after this last statement, and Jude decided he had better leap into action quickly.

'Ho, ho, ho,' he bellowed. 'Ho, ho, ho. Where are the good children who stay here tonight?'

He stomped his feet and stepped into the dayroom in all his Santa glory: splendid red coat and trousers with white fur trimmings; a black belt cinched tight around a large, if fake, belly; round glasses; flowing white beard and all.

The group of children shrieked and whispered in delight. The very young ones looked apprehensive, and the older ones were excited. Some of the children scurried closer to Carrie for comfort and reassurance. The noise roused Maya, who had been sleeping in a little cot to the side, and Carrie swiftly went to pick her up.

'My, my, my,' Jude panted between exaggerated heavy breaths as he pretended to struggle under the weight of his sack. 'You're a long way from Lapland, but I found you.'

He winked at Carrie, but she looked at him blankly and jiggled a still stormy Maya up and down. Evidently she hadn't cottoned on that it was him, Jude, who was sweating under all the Santa paraphernalia. She was probably expecting Ray.

'Where's Lapland?' the little boy Luke cut into Jude's ruminations. 'You live at the North Pole, don't you?'

'Um.' Jude floundered. Had he tripped up in some capacity? He hadn't given Santa's home much consideration in recent years. In the movies, Santa tended to live at the North Pole, but British parents took their kids on mini-breaks to Lapland to meet Santa and his reindeer. How confusing.

He cleared his throat and set down his sack with a thump. 'Well, now, my little friend, that is a really good question. Some say that I *do* live at the North Pole. But others believe I come from Lapland. It doesn't really matter either way, and it's very cold in both places...'

He had talked himself down a dead-end road and faltered. The children regarded him in expectant silence. Jude felt beads of perspiration form on his forehead and resisted the urge to wipe his brow. He hadn't expected the third degree when he let Ray talk him into taking on Santa duties.

During his hesitation, the little girl who thought the Grinch was a softie spoke up. 'But how did you get our letters if we sent them to the wrong place?'

'Ah,' Carrie chimed in. She had sat down again once Maya calmed down. Now she belatedly returned Jude's wink and briefly smiled at him before replying to the little girl. Jude breathed a secret sigh of relief. Help at last.

'You see, Lucy,' Carrie began. 'That would be because of the helpful elves. They collected all the letters and brought them to Father Christmas wherever he was at the time. Whether at the North Pole or in Lapland.'

'Father Christmas?' Several of the children echoed the name and giggled.

'Yes, Father Christmas. Don't you call him that over here?'

'Nah, he's Santa. You know, Santa Claus,' Luke explained earnestly.

'*Of course* he is. *I* remember now.' Carrie spread her hands wide and smiled. 'It's only…' She leaned forward and whispered to the children in a conspiratorial fashion. 'You see, where I come from… You know, in England, we call him Father Christmas. Or Santa, I suppose. But mostly Father Christmas.'

'Really?' The children were agog. 'But it's the same guy, right?'

'Absolutely. It's only a different kind of nickname for him. You know, like Luke could also be called Lukey or Lucky…'

'My parents call me Lou,' Luke offered.

'There you go. See? So Father Christmas, Santa, it's all the same.' Carrie warmed to her theme. 'Sometimes, we even call him St Nick.'

'Hrck-hmm.' Jude cleared his throat, trying to take control of the conversation once more. He was sweating even more heavily in his costume than before, and he was worried he might pass out if he didn't get de-robed and returned to his normal self soon. 'So who's been naughty, and who's been nice?'

The children sat quietly, looking at him with wide eyes. None of them said anything, and one little boy began to cry. Jude gave himself a mental forehead slap. He obviously had a lot to learn about being a convincing Santa. Regarding each child in turn, trying to smile as widely as he could under his enormous fake beard, he eventually spoke again.

'Ah, I see. You've all been wonderfully good. That would explain why my sack is so full.' He rustled the sack and stepped across the room to sit down on an empty chair, dragging his sack behind him as though it were too heavy to carry even another few yards.

'Now, let's see.' Jude retrieved the first present. He studied the label. 'This one is for Sarah-Jane.'

Sarah-Jane turned out to be a little girl in a wheelchair. She gasped with excitement when Santa held up a large, brightly wrapped present. One of the nurses patted her shoulder and walked over to Jude to fetch Sarah-Jane's present for her.

'Can I unwrap it?' the little girl asked eagerly.

'Why, of course.' Jude was all magnanimous indulgence. While Sarah-Jane tore at the wrapping, he continued giving out presents. 'Let's see who's next… Harrison? Where are you?'

A boy of about ten raised his hand. 'That's me.'

'Happy Crimbo, Harrison.' Jude handed the boy's present to a nurse and delved back into the sack, but was stopped by a burst of laughter.

'What did you say?' Luke snorted. 'Happy Crimbo?'

'Err…yes. It means "Happy Christmas" where I come from,' Jude responded, proud of his quick reaction this time round.

'What language do they speak in Lapland?' Luke persisted. 'It sure sounds like English, but it's all weird.'

'I think we're getting Santa in a globe-trotting mood today,' Carrie suggested, springing to the rescue yet again. '"Happy Crimbo" is what they say in the UK, where Maya and I come from. Of course, Santa is travelling all over the world tonight. He'll be speaking German next, or French. Or Spanish. Who knows?'

'Yes, yes,' Jude picked up the idea in his deepest, most resonant Santa voice. 'Frohe Weichnachten. Buon Natale. Feliz Navidad.'

He cast around furiously for seasonal greetings in any other languages.

'Joyeux Noël,' Carrie contributed. 'That's French, by the way.'

'Cool!' Luke was intrigued. 'Can you do Chinese, too?'

'Errr…' Jude was caught out again.

'"Sheng-dan kuai-leh", offered the nurse who had handed Harrison his present. 'At least that's how I think it's pronounced.' She blushed and shrugged. 'My grandparents are Chinese.'

'Yes, yes, well done,' Jude boomed. He debated whether to repeat the phrase but decided against it.

'Luke. *Lou*. You're next, here you go.'

Luke jumped up and took his present from Santa. 'Happy Crimbo, Santa!' He grinned as he tried out the new season's greeting. 'And thank you.'

At this, 'thank you's' echoed all round from the children who had already unwrapped their presents. Sarah-Jane clutched a large ballerina doll on her lap. Harrison was already commanding imaginary armies with his action man figure. Santa had brought books and jigsaw puzzles, construction bricks, and modelling clay. Luke received a secret spaceman mission-diary full of codes and riddles.

'Well, well, well,' Jude proclaimed pompously once his job was done, rising to his feet and wondering idly why he kept speaking like an ancient school teacher. 'I'd better be getting on to visit some more children. I wish you all a very happy Christmas, my friends. Be good now, and don't eat too many sweets.'

'Bye, Santa,' the children shouted as one. They waved and cheered, and, for a moment, every one of them appeared to have forgotten their illnesses. Jude was deeply moved. These children were braver than he could ever have imagined. He was glad now that he had accepted the job of giving out Santa's presents when Ray had suggested it. Somehow, it had reminded him of what Christmas was really about.

He left Carrie and Maya with the children in the dayroom while he went to de-Santa himself. A few minutes later, he returned with Ray in tow. He entered the dayroom, rubbing his chin, which was still itchy from the beard, and beamed.

'Hello, you guys. I'm Jude. I'm with Carrie and Maya. Hey, wow, what's all this?'

He feigned surprise at seeing the heap of torn wrapping paper on the floor and pointed at the children's presents one by one. 'Cor, what have I missed? Has Santa been here?'

The children laughed gleefully. 'He was, he was,' they shouted.

'And he sure talked funny,' Luke immediately elaborated. 'Like, all sorts of weird languages. And he said "Happy Crimbo" to us.'

'Happy Crimbo?' Jude repeated with mock surprise. 'Well, he must have come straight from the UK.'

'He said he was from Lapland,' Sarah-Jane explained. 'Are you from Lapland?'

Jude answered the question seriously. 'No, I'm not, sweetheart. I'm from England. Although that is a lot nearer to Lapland than New York is.'

'What's next?' Luke prompted impatiently. 'We've got to do something, or else the nurses will tell us to go to bed.'

'How about we sing some songs?' Carrie suggested. 'It *is* Christmas Eve. You've got to sing songs on Christmas Eve!'

'Oh yes!' the children screamed with excitement. The sudden burst of noise startled Maya, who burst into tears. Carrie bounced her up and down on her knees to calm her down.

'What shall we sing, Maya sweets?' she spoke to her daughter but addressed all the children at the same time. 'What's your favourite song?'

The children responded with vehement shouts.

'Frosty the Snowman!'

'Jingle Bells!'

'Santa Claus Is Coming To Town!'

Jude laughed. 'What a collection of songs. Okay, here goes!'

He launched into the opening line of 'Jingle Bells', and the children, Carrie, and the nurses joined in quickly, clapping hands and stamping feet if they could.

'I want "Santa Claus Is Coming To Town" next,' Luke bellowed before the last word of 'Jingle Bells' had even faded.

'Yes, yes, yes,' the other kids agreed eagerly.

Jude scratched his head. 'It's a cool song, but it's hard to do without a guitar.'

'You play the guitar?' Luke pounced.

Jude shrugged. 'A little.'

Carrie snorted, but Jude ignored her.

'Cool,' Luke exclaimed. 'There's a guitar in the music room. Can we get it, Nurse Joan? Please?'

'Sure,' the nurse agreed. 'Why not? That's what it's there for, after all.'

Luke turned to Jude and grinned widely. 'We do a lot of music therapy. It's meant to make us feel better.'

'Ah.' Jude nodded knowledgeably. 'That makes sense. Music always makes me feel better, too.'

The nurse returned laden with instruments. She had brought the guitar, but also a few tambourines, triangles, and a couple of small drums. She handed the guitar to Jude and the percussion instruments to the kids.

Jude took the guitar and looked at it approvingly. It was a nice make, recently re-strung and obviously well loved. He set about tuning it, oblivious to the kids watching his every move.

'He looks like a pro,' Luke commented to Carrie.

'He plays quite a bit,' Carrie whispered. 'But don't tell him I said that, or he'll get embarrassed.'

Jude shot her a look, and she grinned at him sweetly. He finished tuning and got to his feet, placing the strap of the guitar round his neck and shoulder.

'Right, band, are you ready?' he challenged the percussionists, and everybody acquiesced eagerly.

'Okay... Here we go. A-one...a-two...a-one-two-three-four...'

Jude's voice filled the little dayroom, and for an instant, the children were too stunned to join in. Jude strummed and sang, pivoting in a slow circle to face all the kids in turn as he performed, and a great cheer rose.

'This dude is *awesome*,' Luke enthused. 'Wow.'

'Come on, everybody, join in with me,' Jude ad-libbed between verses, and the kids needed no further encouragement. Their soft voices mingled beautifully with Jude's trained one, and, after a few seconds, the first tentative beats on the drum started to mark the rhythm of the song. Carrie clapped her hands to help keep time, and the dayroom transformed into an impromptu stage with a small choir of children singing with enthusiasm and joy.

They had such a great time that they did the song twice more before moving on to 'Frosty', and none of the performers noticed a small gathering of nurses and duty doctors by the door.

'One more, one more,' the kids begged when the latest song came to an end. However, Luke, the most enthusiastic of singers, had paled and sunk onto a chair, wheezing and clutching his chest. He seemed exhausted. Nurse Joan was at his side, holding his hand and taking his pulse.

'I don't know,' she muttered doubtfully. 'I think perhaps you've all had enough.'

'Oh, *no*,' the children wailed, Luke included. 'Just one more. Please?'

The duty doctor at the door relented. 'Okay, guys, because it's Christmas. *One* more. But you let Jude sing on his own now and listen. Special treat. If that's all right with Jude, that is?'

'Um…of course. If that's what you want.' Jude smiled and took a little bow. 'I don't want to push it too far.'

The doctor smiled. 'I think the kids can handle one more song before their Christmas feast—'

'Christmas feast?' The children latched onto this notion instantly and screamed with excitement. One of the nurses rolled her eyes and elbowed the doctor good-naturedly in the side.

'Trust Doctor to give away the secret,' she laughed. 'But shush now, let's have that last song, and then you can have a little feast.'

'Wow,' Sarah-Jane cheered. 'This is, like, the best Christmas *ever!* And I thought Christmas would suck this year.'

The other kids nodded their agreement, and the nurses looked both wistful and stricken. Nobody quite knew what to say, so Jude struck a chord on the guitar and stepped into the centre of the room once more.

'Well, there's only one song that fits,' he announced. 'You stay put, and Carrie and I'll do the rocking for you.'

He summoned Carrie to join him. Carrie looked flustered, but he mouthed his encouragement at her. 'Come on, it'll be okay.'

The kids cheered and clapped, so Carrie got to her feet. She handed Maya to one of the nurses and stood next to Jude awkwardly.

'What are you doing, you oaf?' she whispered.

'We're going to do some rocking around the Christmas tree,' Jude stage-whispered back, 'and I need a backing voice.'

'Ah.' Carrie swallowed. 'I see.'

'Pretend we're at home,' Jude continued, his voice slightly lower now so the children wouldn't hear.

'I'm not sure *stripping* is appropriate under the circumstances,' Carrie breathed into his ear.

Jude chortled. 'Probably not, but everything else goes. C'mon, let's roll.'

So Jude and Carrie did a spirited rendition of one of their favourite classic Christmas rock 'n' roll tunes, and while the kids didn't join in with the singing, they clapped their hands and nodded their heads. They also gave Jude and Carrie a great round of applause when the song finished, and Jude offered an exaggerated bow.

'My pleasure,' he laughed, thoroughly at ease now.

'You remind me of someone,' one of the nurses suddenly said.

Jude looked at her and smiled. He tried to head off her recognition at the pass. 'Really? I don't think so. I'm an ordinary kind of guy.'

'Oh no, you're not,' the nurse persisted. '*I* know. You're Jude Shaw. My sister saw you in concert the other night, with Tuscq, and she's been obsessed with you ever since. She got your album and everything!'

A stunned silence greeted this announcement. Jude ran a hand through his hair, unsure how to react. Normally he would pull the suave rock star act, but it didn't seem appropriate in this setting. He swallowed and shrugged and smiled all at the same time.

'Oh my gawd—he's a rock star,' Luke diagnosed. 'A real rock star, right here at the hospital!'

'Is that right, Jude?' Ray wanted to know. Jude gave a start. He had completely forgotten about the Italian policeman. 'Are you a rock star?'

'Well,' Jude shrugged some more. 'Maybe not quite a rock *star*. You know, I'm not famous or anything. But I do play in a band, that's right.'

'Here he is, on stage,' the young nurse exclaimed excitedly. 'My sister took a video at the concert. Look at him go. He's a rock star all right!'

She held up a tablet and played a video of Jude and The Blood Roses performing their encore at the New York gig with Tuscq. On the tiny screen, Jude was strutting his stuff and playing to the audience, getting them to clap and cheer and sing along. They were eating out of his hands.

Jude remembered the moment well. It had been a rousing end to a fantastic tour, but he had never in a million years considered that it would put him on the spot in front of a gathering of young children in a hospital in the Big Apple on Christmas Eve.

'I suppose that *is* me,' he conceded.

He couldn't quite work out why this admission should feel so awkward. Perhaps it was because his quest for fame and fortune seemed a little hollow under the circumstances.

'That is so cool!' Luke announced, his eyes flicking from the video to the real Jude and back.

Jude finally found his voice again. 'I told you I like music,' he grinned. 'What can I say? I love to rock.'

'What on earth brings you here of all places?' the doctor wanted to know. 'Shouldn't you be somewhere? A party, maybe? Or even at home?'

'Well, yeah. That's a long story.' Jude smiled. 'I'd have to say that it's the spirit of Christmas that brought

Carrie and me, and, of course our daughter Maya, here today. It's rather a long story.'

'You never said anything about being a rock star when you rented my brother's apartment,' Ray remarked drolly. 'He'll be tickled pink when he finds out. He'll probably rename the place "The Rock Star Suite" and charge triple for it from now on. I can already see the plaque on the building. "Jude Shaw stayed here".' He laughed explosively, and everybody joined in.

Suddenly, the awkward moment passed, and the senior nurse clapped her hands. 'Come on, you kids, we've laid on a little feast for you. It *is* Christmas Eve after all!'

Among great whoops of joy, the kids that could walk unaided got to their feet and followed the senior nurse out of the dayroom. The others were wheeled by nurses. Luke, however, walked across to Jude. He looked at the rock star earnestly.

'Will you stay with us for the feast?'

Jude raised his eyebrows and knelt down to bring his face level with the little boy. 'I'd love to, Luke, but I don't think that'll work. There might not be enough food, you see, and I can't gatecrash the party.'

'But you're a rock star,' Luke objected. 'You're supposed to be gatecrashing parties. You can be our star guest!' He took Jude's hand and tugged eagerly. 'C'mon, I'm sure it'll be fine.'

Jude shot Carrie a look, but she shrugged helplessly. 'I don't know what to do,' she mouthed.

'Ah, come on, you guys, I'm sure there'll be plenty,' Ray offered his opinion. 'Besides, you don't have to eat much, do you? The kids would love the company. They'll never forget this.'

'Too right,' the senior nurse confirmed. 'We'd love you to stay. All the staff are tucking in too. We're trying to give the kids a little semblance of normality with a big "family" meal. There's easily enough for everyone.'

'Well, if you're sure?' Jude and Carrie exchanged a glance. 'We'd love to.'

And so Jude, Carrie, and Maya sat down for a proper Christmas Eve dinner after all. The hospital staff had arranged a long table in the canteen and, as the senior nurse said, all the nurses and doctors on duty were sitting down with the children to have a festive meal. There was ham, roast potatoes and mash, gravy, sausages, and stuffing. In deference to poorly little taste buds, there were also fries, potato chips, tomato ketchup, breaded chicken nuggets, pizza bites, dough balls, and spaghetti. Everyone drank juice or water, but there was hot chocolate to go with pudding.

Jude and Carrie were given the place of honour at the centre of the table. Maya sat on Carrie's lap and happily tried mashed potato with gravy and a few mushed up vegetables. Even though it was way after the little girl's bedtime, she was on top form after her late nap, and Carrie and Jude were all too happy to enjoy the moment rather than worrying about their daughter's customary routine.

'I don't believe this,' Carrie whispered to Jude. 'At lunch time, I thought we'd be roughing it, and that Christmas would be a complete disaster. I was tearful and miserable and worried. And yet here we are, a mere few hours later, having had a marvellous celebration, having shared out presents, and being fed like kings and queens.'

'I know,' Jude replied. 'It's unbelievable. I can't wrap my head around what's happened to us today.' He took a sip of his drink while he gathered his thoughts. 'You know, I feel humbled by everyone's generosity. We're perfect strangers, and they've taken us in and are sharing their Christmas Eve with us. I never thought I'd find so much… I don't know, fulfilment? Cheer? Satisfaction? Whatever, I never thought it could be so magical to spend a few hours with children in a hospital. I never knew that simply *being* there for them, singing songs and playing games, would make such a difference, but… I'd have to agree with Sarah-Jane. This is shaping up to be the best Christmas Eve ever.'

~ 6 ~

All I Want for Christmas

'Shhh,' Carrie whispered sleepily. 'Don't wake Maya.'

'I won't,' Jude promised. 'I only want to see what it's like out there.'

He slid out of bed and shivered. It was very cold. He wrapped his arms around himself as he padded towards the window and peeked through the curtain. It was still dark, but he could see that snow had drifted high on the roads and sidewalks. Little caps of white adorned the window ledges and fire escapes of the buildings opposite. Jude shook his head. There was no way that they would return to London that day, either.

He closed the curtains and crawled back under the duvet, snuggling close to Carrie for warmth and comfort.

'Merry Christmas,' he breathed into her ear.

'Merry Christmas, darling,' Carrie replied softly. 'Is it bad out there?'

'The worst. It snowed all night, and it's still coming down.'

'We're not going home today?'

'I doubt it. I'll ring the airline in a little minute.'

'Do it now. At least then we know.' Carrie sounded impatient and wistful at the same time.

'You sure?' Jude felt reluctant to climb out of bed again to find his mobile phone. The duvet was warm, and he was still basking in the happy afterglow of the events of the previous evening. Finding a place to stay, going to church, celebrating at the hospital, and making love to Carrie, quietly, gently, after they had finally settled Maya into the dresser drawer that they had transformed into a makeshift little cot.

'Not quite a manger,' Jude had joked while he had padded the drawer with blankets, 'but not far off.'

'Thank God she's still so tiny,' Carrie had concurred. 'Another couple of months, and this wouldn't have been an option.'

All in all, while unusual, their Christmas Eve had been more festive and more appropriate, somehow more in the spirit of the season, than he had ever experienced before. After all that, he simply wasn't ready to collide head-on with reality via an unhappy exchange with airline staff.

'Please?' Carrie persisted gently. 'I hate not knowing.'

'All right. You wait here for me, though. Don't get up.'

Jude dragged himself out of bed again and put on his jumper to ward off the cold. He tiptoed towards the kitchen area and turned to face away from the main bedroom so that his voice wouldn't wake up his sleeping daughter. In the event, his precaution proved unnecessary. He didn't even get to speak with anyone. The airline was running an automated reply service, and the message was unequivocal. Jude sighed and hung up. He kept his jumper on when he returned to cuddle with Carrie once more.

'And?'

'The airport is closed. Nobody is answering the phones at the airline. There's an automated message saying that owing to inclement weather, JFK airport is closed until further notice, and that passengers will be notified by text or email when the situation improves. That's it.'

Carrie sighed. 'I guessed as much.'

'Well, considering the amount of snow out there, it's hardly a surprise.' Jude was philosophical about their situation.

'I know. It's just… It feels like we're never gonna get home.'

'We will.' Jude was firm on this fact. 'Of course we will. Once it stops snowing, they'll clear the runways and get things back to normal. I'm certain the wind has dropped a little. It's bound to blow itself out. You'll see, we'll get on a plane tomorrow.'

'I hope so.' Carrie yawned and stretched. Jude watched her with loving eyes. His girlfriend. His soulmate. Mother to his adorable daughter. He loved her more than he could ever say.

'I love you, babes,' he whispered.

'I love you too, Jude.' Carrie smiled.

Jude fixed her eyes with his gaze until she blinked. Idly, he picked up a lock of her hair and wound it around his fingers.

'You're so beautiful.'

Carrie tittered. 'So you said last night.'

'That's because I mean it. I marvel every day that you're my girl.'

Carrie blushed. 'Thank you. I feel the same way.'

Jude snuggled closer to her. 'Do you think we have enough time for—you know?'

Carrie raised her head to take a peek at their daughter. Then she picked up her wristwatch from the nightstand to take a look at the time. She shook her head.

'I don't think so, lover boy.'

'Too bad. You sure? A really quick one, maybe?' Jude nibbled at her ear and stroked her breast. Carrie snorted and pushed his hand away.

'No,' she whispered emphatically. 'I can guarantee that Maya will wake up halfway through.'

'So? She won't know what we're doing,' Jude objected softly. It didn't seem a big deal to him. Their daughter was so little, and she often lay cooing and singing in her cot for quite some time before demanding her parents' attention in the morning.

'You don't know that,' Carrie hissed. 'We might traumatise her for life.'

'Rubbish,' Jude chuckled, but he relented. On balance, it probably wasn't such a good idea. 'Rain check until tonight?'

'Snow check, under the circumstances,' Carrie joked. 'But okay. So…' She inhaled deeply and stretched her hands above her head. 'What are we going to do today? It *is* Christmas proper now. I'm afraid I haven't got your present here. And the food selection for our feast is still as it was yesterday afternoon before we went to church, although I suppose...'

'Marry me.' Jude cut into Carrie's reflection, surprising himself as much as her.

'What?'

'Marry me, Carrie.'

'Are you proposing to me after all this time?' Carrie smiled to soften her words, but her face was the picture of disbelief.

'I am, I suppose. I hadn't thought about it like that. I simply want you to be my wife.' He laughed uncertainly. 'You know. *Mrs Carrie Shaw.*'

'Why now?' Carrie sat up and pushed her hair out of her face. It stuck up in adorable dishevelled strands, and Jude forcefully resisted the urge to stroke it.

'Because... Well, because I want to make it official. It's long overdue, but there hasn't been a good time. You know, the baby, the tour...'

'Wow.' Carrie sighed. 'I'm stunned.'

'So am I. But I'll ask again, if you want.'

Carrie giggled. 'Go on.'

Jude swallowed. He wriggled himself into an upright position and crouched awkwardly on one knee right there on the bed. The mattress sagged and the springs squeaked in protest, but he found a stable position and balanced his body carefully. Then he took Carrie's hand in his and looked her in the eyes.

'Carrie Collins, will you marry me?'

For a seemingly interminable moment, Carrie didn't reply, and Jude found himself holding his breath. Finally, her answer came.

'Yes, I will. Of course I will, Jude.'

She reached out her hands and put them around his neck, pulling him bodily down towards her to give him a kiss.

'Great. Fantastic. Wow. Thanks! Hooray!' Jude issued the first random words that came into his head. They giggled and kissed, and giggled and kissed some more. Jude felt like a great weight had been lifted. Finally, finally, he was making things properly right. And she had said yes! He smiled and beamed and punched the air.

Carrie shook her head. 'God help me, tying my fate forever to an overgrown bad boy, but yes, I love you, and I'd be honoured to be your wife. I suppose it's too late to plan a spring wedding, but maybe in the summer…'

Jude stopped in his euphoric air-punching and froze. For a moment, he didn't know what to say, but suddenly he felt his face split into a huge grin.

'Today. Let's get married today.'

'*Today?*' Carrie squeaked in shock. 'What, here? Today? Without any of our friends or family? With no dress? On Christmas Day? In *New York?*'

Jude faltered, but only briefly. 'And why not? I know, when you put it like that, it sounds preposterous. But wouldn't it be so *romantic?* I mean, what else are we going to do? Sit around and twiddle our thumbs?'

'We could *plan* our wedding,' Carrie suggested mildly.

'Planning is highly overrated,' Jude pronounced loftily. He saw Carrie's face fall, and in an instant he understood. The dress, the party, the fun. That was important to her. He had another idea.

'Look, tell you what. If we get married today, here, right now... Then how about we have a big party, dress, guests, reception, and all, at home in the summer? It could be...' Jude scrunched up his forehead, trying to remember the right term for the occasion he had in mind. 'A blessing. That's it. We could have a blessing ceremony for this wedding of ours that took place in New York.'

Jude increasingly warmed to his theme. 'Wouldn't that be the best of both worlds? Think about it. What a story! Imagine when we get to tell Maya all about it, or our grandkids...'

'Well—wow.' Carrie was stunned. 'I suppose it would be very romantic...' She smiled but frowned at the same time. 'How would we pull it off, though? I mean, this isn't Vegas, and Fifth Avenue isn't exactly lined with wedding chapels.'

'No idea.' Jude wafted his hands about airily. 'But I've a good feeling about this, like it's meant to be. We've got a church next door. There's bound to be a service this morning. Let's go in and ask.'

'You're officially nuts,' Carrie snorted. 'But okay. Why not? It could be an adventure, I suppose.'

'I'm serious,' Jude quietly reiterated. 'Don't go along with it because you don't think it'll work out. I mean it. I want to marry you today.'

Carrie paused for a moment, looking distinctly guilty. But she rallied and laughed. 'Okay, you got me. Guilty as charged.' She spread her hands wide and erupted in peals of laughter. Her voice sounded happy and excited. 'I surrender myself to fate. I'm in your hands. I trust you. If we can work it out, it was meant to be. Let's go for it.'

'Really?'

'Really.'

'Yay! But, oh, oh, Carrie…' Jude's enthusiasm waned. 'I haven't even got a ring! I mean, I do, of course I do, but it's at home, waiting for the right time…' Jude grinned ruefully. 'I'm sorry! Badly thought-out plan of mine.'

'I don't care about the ring,' Carrie soothed. 'That's a detail. Although I suppose we'll—'

She never got to finish her sentence because Maya chose that moment to wake up and announce her presence. Jude and Carrie turned simultaneously to look at their irate offspring, and Jude recovered first.

'I think she's grumpy.'

'I bet she's hungry,' Carrie supplied. 'Time to get up, Romeo.'

So they rose and prepared a simple breakfast using the random foodstuffs that Jude had obtained the previous day. Neither of them mentioned the 'W' word during the morning, but the idea, the plan, the vision hung between them like a lucky charm. It enveloped them in a golden bubble, and every little gesture, every word, every action seemed to be loaded with significance.

At just before ten o'clock, the church bells started ringing again. Jude and Carrie exchanged a glance, and Jude raised his hand for a tentative high-five.

'This is it,' he exclaimed. 'Let's see if we can make it happen.'

Carrie accepted the high-five, and Maya gurgled at her parents' strange antics. Jude scurried around to collect everything he thought they might need, including wallets, passports, and their entry visas. 'There's bound to be paperwork,' he declared. 'Best be prepared.'

Carrie shrugged and agreed. Within a few minutes, the little family bundled up warm and ventured outside, all essentials safely contained in Carrie's rucksack. It was still snowing, but less heavily so. The sky was grey and low, and the air was bitterly cold, but the wind had dropped. They bustled hurriedly towards the church, purpose in every movement.

'I feel like I'm being pulled on a drawstring,' Carrie gasped.

'I know what you mean,' Jude replied, panting to keep pace with his fiancée while carrying their daughter. 'I sense a certain urgency in your step.'

Carrie laughed. 'Of course you do. You planted this ridiculous idea in my head, and now I want it as badly as you do. Oh, here we go.'

They had arrived at the church once more. Today, the door stood wide open.

'I'm nervous,' Carrie confessed. 'What are we going to do next? What if they think we're mad?'

'We *are* mad,' Jude deadpanned. 'That's why I know this is right. Let's go in and see what happens.'

He took Carrie's hand, and they stepped into the church. The warmth and the candlelight welcomed them as they had the previous afternoon. As before, the organ was playing softly, and there was a general hum of conversation before the service.

Jude looked round. 'Let's find the minister.'

Carrie swallowed. 'Okay. Tell me why I'm nervous like a truant teenager?'

'No idea,' Jude laughed. 'Did you ever play truant and go to church?'

'Of course not,' Carrie huffed.

'So there's no reason why you should feel this way.'

'You know what I mean!'

'Of course I do. I'm only making light of it so you don't chicken out on me. C'mon, let's walk.'

They took a few hesitant steps down the aisle, looking around for somebody official to help them. They didn't find the minister, but they did find Ray.

'Yo! Carrie! Jude! Merry Christmas!' Ray's voice rang out through the entire church, and his body followed the sound like a heat-seeking missile. He wrapped Carrie in a big hug before she had even had time to open her mouth.

'I'm so happy to see you here,' Ray boomed. Jude squirmed, aware that they were the centre of attention for anyone there.

'Merry Christmas,' Carrie eventually responded and earned herself another hug.

'Merry Christmas,' Jude echoed. Ray examined him critically.

'Hey, what's the matter with you, man? You look miserable.'

'I do?' Jude was aghast.

'You do.'

'Not so much miserable as nervous, I should think,' Carrie offered from the side.

'Nervous? Why would he be nervous?' Ray was intrigued.

'You see…' Carrie began.

'It's just…' Jude said at the same time.

'What's up?' Ray quipped. 'Are you guys on the run from someone?'

Jude flinched, and Carrie grinned. Ray instantly homed in on their reaction. He lowered his voice. 'Are you on the run? Have you eloped?'

'No, of course not,' Jude finally choked a reply. 'We're not on the run.'

'And we haven't eloped, but…' Carrie faltered.

'But what? Guys? What is it?'

'Um. Well.' Jude shifted from foot to foot. 'You'll think we're nuts.'

'After last night? Nah. Never. Jude, my rock star friend, spill the beans. What's eatin' you?'

'You see…' Jude smiled broadly. 'We decided this morning to get married.' There. It was out. Jude breathed a sigh of relief. That had been quite easy.

Ray looked from Jude to Carrie and back, taking in Maya along the way. 'You're not married already?'

'Um, no.' Jude paused, unsure whether more information was needed. Confronted with Ray's inquisitive eyes, he surmised that it was. 'We fell pregnant before we had a chance to get married, and next there was the tour…'

'Of course, of course.' Ray nodded his understanding. 'And now you've decided to make it official. Congratulations, guys.' He slapped Jude heartily on the back. 'When's the date?'

'Err, well. We thought—'

'Today,' Carrie cut into Jude's stammering response. 'We want to get married today.'

'*Today?*' Ray's reaction mirrored Carrie's initial response perfectly, Jude noted. Maybe he was mad after all. Nonetheless, he shrugged.

'Yes, today. Do you think it's possible?'

'Well, now…' Ray rubbed his forehead. 'I think it's impossibly romantic,' he offered. 'As for *possible*…'

'Please don't say it's not,' Carrie begged.

'I'm not saying anything,' Ray replied. 'I'm thinking. You see, to get married in New York, you have to fill in some paperwork. Always assuming you've got your passports and visas in order, which I'm sure you do.'

He stared a challenge at Jude and Carrie, who nodded obligingly.

'Good, good,' Ray continued. 'Ah, the marriage license… That's gotta be filled in at the City Clerk's Office, which is closed today, of course. And, also, it normally needs to be filled in at least twenty-four hours in advance of the actual ceremony.'

Carrie's face crumpled. 'Oh, no. That's no good. We haven't got the form or the twenty-four hours.'

Jude hugged her tightly when he saw tears brimming in her eyes. Damn him and his foolish notion. He should have known better.

'Leave it with me,' Ray ordered. 'Sit. Right here.' He pointed at a pew. 'Give me five minutes. I have an idea.'

And he bustled off before either Jude or Carrie could react.

A short time later, they saw Ray talking animatedly to the minister from the night before. He pointed in their direction and waved. Jude waved back, and the minister half smiled. Ray kept talking, using his hands to emphasise points, and the minister's features gradually relaxed. The two men shook hands, and Ray scuttled off to talk to another man in the congregation. More gesturing and waving ensued, and Jude began to feel slightly self-conscious. What the heck was Ray doing on their behalf?

'I got it all sorted,' Ray declared a mere five minutes later. 'You're gettin' married today. Come and meet the minister. It's all a bit rush-rush because the service is due to start, but he'll tie it all together. I'm sure these good folks here will be delighted to add a wedding to the Christmas Day service. But come with me, you've gotta fill in the paperwork.'

'You what? Wow! How?' Jude struggled to get a word in edgewise, but the thoroughly overexcited Ray didn't pause for breath.

'I'll explain, c'mon, trust me.'

So Jude, Carrie, and Maya followed Ray to the vestry, where the minister and the other man were waiting for them.

'Father John, meet Jude and Carrie.' Ray hesitated briefly. 'And Maya, of course.'

Father John inclined his head and smiled. He regarded the little family silently. His deep blue eyes were kind but probing. Jude felt as though Father John was looking right into his soul, and he shivered. He hoped he wouldn't be found wanting.

'So you want to get married today, of all days?' Father John finally spoke.

'That's right.' Jude and Carrie replied at the same time, and Jude took Carrie's hand for comfort and reassurance. Father John seemed to notice the gesture, and he nodded.

'May I ask why? It appears you've already explored your union.'

Carrie blushed deeply, and Jude cringed. Put like that, it sounded very sordid.

'Don't get me wrong, I don't disapprove of your desire to enter holy matrimony. But it is my duty to understand why you want to enter this bond when you have already…evidently…bonded.'

'Ah. Well.' Jude swallowed. 'We—um. We hit a rough patch last year, and we nearly…lost each other. So to speak.'

'Jude didn't know I was expecting,' Carrie offered shyly. 'To be honest, I didn't realise at first. And then…'

'…then we got back together, thankfully, because I love this woman with all my heart.' Jude wrapped an arm around Carrie and blinked to hold back the tears that unexpectedly pricked in his eyes. 'We talked about a wedding, but…'

'…I didn't feel comfortable getting married while pregnant,' Carrie explained. 'It didn't seem right. I didn't want it to look like we got married because we "had" to. What we have…our love, it's stronger than that.'

She reached up and planted a little kiss on Jude's cheek. Jude reeled. He had never heard Carrie voice these thoughts before. He had always assumed that her reasons were more practical, to do with dresses and partying. He pulled her close again and leaned his head against hers.

'And so here we are,' he finished off Carrie's thoughts.

'Yes, yes.' Father John was calm and reflective. 'I can see that. And I understand your story. But why today? Why not wait until you get home to your native country?'

'Why not today?' Jude simply challenged. 'It feels right. I don't know why.'

'Are you regular church goers?'

'We haven't been, no.' Carrie evidently thought that brutal honesty was the way forward. 'But we came here yesterday, and...it was... I don't know. Like fate. A lot of things happened yesterday. Things that really moved us.'

'So I hear.' Father John shot a meaningful glance at Ray, who beamed like the Cheshire cat.

'Okay. So be it. The Lord works in mysterious ways, and he has brought you here today. So yes, I will marry you both.'

'But Ray said something about papers and twenty-four hours?' Despite the minister's agreement, Jude didn't dare to get his hopes up.

'Well.' Father John now smiled broadly. 'As an authorised minister, of course I have my own stash of licenses that you can fill in right here, always assuming you have your passports and visas, and...' He coughed, embarrassed. 'The small matter of the thirty-five dollar fee.'

'Yes, we have all that,' Carrie quickly confirmed.

'Good. As for the twenty-four hour requirement...'

Jude's heart sank to the bottom of his feet. He felt like he was on a rollercoaster, up one moment, down the next. What game were the minister and Ray playing with them?

'I can help with that.' The mysterious second man spoke up.

'You can?' Jude was agog.

'You see,' Ray cut in, 'you see, you can get around the twenty-four hours with a judicial waiver. And my friend Warren here, he's a judge.'

'You can?' Carrie repeated Ray's words. 'You are?'

'I sure am, Miss,' the judge spoke up. 'And if Father John is happy to conduct the marriage ceremony, I'm happy to facilitate the paperwork. But you must file these papers with the City Clerk's Office tomorrow. In person, together, and at the same time.'

'We'll do that,' Jude agreed. 'So what you're saying is…' He squeezed Carrie's hand again. 'We really can get married today?'

'Yes, if you so wish.'

'We do.' Carrie spoke resolutely.

'Right. Let's do this.' Father John rubbed his hands together energetically. 'I'll go and make a brief announcement. We'll add your nuptials to the end of the service. That gives it a greater sense of occasion too. You fill in the paperwork with Warren, and I'll see you out there. Ray and Warren can be your witnesses. Follow my lead.'

He offered his hands for Jude and Carrie to shake before he bustled out.

'Oh my God, Jude, we're getting married,' Carrie whooped with joy. Warren and Ray clapped, and Jude kissed his bride. Abruptly, his face darkened.

'There's only one other problem,' he said. 'We don't have rings, not here.'

'Oh, yes. I remember.' Carrie looked stricken.

'Oh.' Ray looked equally stricken.

Judge Warren was unperturbed. 'You don't legally need a ring,' he offered.

'We don't?'

'You don't.'

'Hm.' Jude wasn't convinced. 'Are you sure?'

'Of course I'm sure.'

'Well... But...'

'I know!' Ray thrust a hand in the air. 'Leave it with me. They'll be cheap and made of plastic, but you'll have rings for today. I'll be back in a couple of minutes.' And he rushed out.

'What's he doing now?' Carrie was flabbergasted. 'Where's he going?'

'No idea,' Judge Warren confessed. 'But Ray's pretty resourceful. I've known him for years. Now, let's get started on that paperwork.'

~ 7 ~

Silver Bells

'Pssst. *Pssst.*' An unfamiliar woman slid herself into the pew to stand next to Carrie. She tugged at her sleeve. 'Carrie!'

Carrie gave a start, and Jude leaned forward curiously to see what was going on.

'I'm Bella,' the woman hissed. 'I'm Ray's wife. Come with me.'

Carrie and Jude exchanged a glance. The Christmas service was in full swing, and the congregation was in the middle of a rousing rendition of 'O Come, All Ye Faithful'. Everybody stood. If they had to leave, now would be a good time.

Bella was already sidestepping back out of the pew, and Jude nudged Carrie to follow her.

'What's going on?' he whispered once they were standing in the side aisle.

'We got something for you,' Bella replied. 'In the vestry. Come on.' And she rushed off, leading the way.

'What now?' Carrie breathed in Jude's ear.

'No idea. We'll see.'

'Ta-da!' Bella closed the door to the vestry with a flourish and twirled Carrie around to face another woman.

'This is my mother, Maria. *Mamma*, this is Carrie, the bride. Carrie, here's your dress.'

'My what?' Carrie repeated, clearly confused. Maria lifted a white bridal gown off the table and held it up for Carrie to examine. She spoke in a thick, lilting Italian accent.

'It may not be your style, but is better than no dress at all, no? I think is your size.'

Carrie looked at Jude and at the dress. She touched the material gingerly, as though expecting it to vanish. Jude was choked with emotion. What a lovely gesture! He wondered if Carrie would accept it.

'I...' Carrie started to speak. She swallowed hard and wiped at her eyes. 'I don't know what to say.'

'It's not perfect,' Bella gushed, 'we know that, but we figured it would be nicer to get married in "a" dress than in...um...jeans. No offense.'

'But... I can't... I don't know if I can...'

'It's only a loan. It's my grandmother's. My mum here wore it, as did I. It can be your "something borrowed". We have a veil too, if you like.' She reached under the table and retrieved a long, flouncy, full-length veil. 'You put it on, do your thing, and give it back. *Nessun problema. Va bene.*'

'Are you sure? Because... Wow, that would be awesome.' Carrie broke into a huge smile, and Jude's heart soared with excitement for her. His beautiful bride would wear a proper gown on her big day! But he didn't get a chance to relish the emotion as Maria briskly addressed herself to him.

'As for you, young man, this is for you.' She thrust a formal suit into Jude's hand. 'Is Ray's. Should fit you.'

Jude raised his eyebrows in surprise and instinctively took a step backwards. *A suit, for him? On loan?* He wasn't at all sure how he felt about that.

As he was still carrying Maya, he bounced her up and down and blessed the momentary reprieve while he figured out how to respond. But Bella burst out laughing and held out her arms to take Maya off him.

'Hello, beautiful,' she cooed. Maya eyed her doubtfully and looked ready to cry, but her gaze locked onto the shiny necklace around Bella's neck. She wrapped her fingers around it and snuggled into Bella's shoulder.

'There you are, my sweet, you play with that,' Bella encouraged. 'You'll stay with auntie Bella while your mummy and daddy get married, won't you?'

Carrie sighed with relief. 'Oh, would you do that, Bella? I hadn't even thought about what to do with Maya during the ceremony. I know it'll be short and... Well, I guessed we'd hold her.'

'Ah, but that was before you had a dress,' Bella laughed. 'It's okay, we'll be fine, won't be, Maya?' She tickled the little girl under her chin, and Maya gurgled happily.

'She should be okay,' Carrie assured Bella. 'She's got a new nappy...a fresh diaper, and she won't need feeding, and...'

'It's okay,' Bella reiterated. 'We'll be fine. Now you guys get dressed.' She looked meaningfully at the suit.

Jude examined it sceptically. Ray was a little shorter than he was, and he doubted that the trousers would even reach down to his ankles.

'It's okay,' Bella laughed once more. 'Ray has very short legs, so we had to take the trouser legs up for him. I've unstitched the hem again, so the legs should be long enough for you. Have a try.'

Now it was Jude's turn to feel a little flustered, but he stamped on his discomfort for Carrie's sake. He was being too British. If his bride wore a borrowed dress, he would jolly well wear a borrowed suit. He smiled widely.

'Okay. Thank you! Where can I…?' He looked around for somewhere to change into his wedding attire.

'Through there, I suppose.' Bella pointed at a door in the corner with her free arm. 'Father John gets changed in there. But don't touch anything.'

'I wouldn't dream of it,' Jude assured her. He took the suit and locked himself into the room.

When he emerged five minutes later, fully suited and feeling quite ready to tie the knot, the sight of Carrie took his breath away. His bride was encased in a beautiful flowing white gown that, miraculously, seemed to fit her perfectly. The veil was pinned into her hair with glittery clips, and she clasped a small bouquet of bright red flowers in her right hand.

'You're so beautiful,' Jude exclaimed. 'This is… It's amazing. The dress fits, and the flowers are lovely…'

Carrie laughed. 'The dress fits because Maria stitched me into it. And the flowers are poinsettias. Maria ransacked one of the floral arrangements from the back of the church.'

'Oh. Wow. I see.' Jude was momentarily speechless. 'I can't believe you guys would go to all this trouble for two strangers.'

'Is nothing,' Maria boomed. 'We love a good wedding, and we love a good story. This is the story of the decade.'

'Oh yes, mum will dine out on this for years to come. But we should go. The service must soon be drawing to a close. It's almost your turn.'

'Where's Ray?' Jude asked. 'He was going to find a ring.'

'He's a-comin',' Maria assured him. She made shooing gestures with her hands. 'Only a few more minutes. *Andiamo, andiamo.*'

'Hurry up,' Bella translated. 'She's right. Let's go. Jude, you turn right as we leave the vestry and go to the front. Warren is waiting for you already. Carrie, you go to the back of the church and prepare to walk down the aisle. Okay?'

'Okay,' Jude and Carrie echoed together, surrendering themselves to the master plan of organisation that had come into operation on their behalf.

They entered the nave to the sound of 'Hark! The Herald Angels Sing', which Jude remembered was the last hymn on the service sheet. It appeared that the Christmas festivities had nearly concluded. This also meant that his wedding was imminent. He felt dizzy with excitement, and his heart beat fast in his chest.

He watched Carrie as she tiptoed along the side aisle towards the back of the church. A lump of emotion—happiness, elation, a tickly feeling of surreality—bubbled up from his tummy and lodged in his throat. A mere three hours ago, he had hatched the grand idea of getting married today. Now, he was in a church, wearing a suit, and finding himself in the hands of compassionate, kind, and very keen strangers who took his dream and turned it into a reality, suit, dress, and all.

'If you saw it in a movie, you'd clap and cheer and completely ignore the fact that this would *never* happen in real life,' he thought. 'And yet here I am.'

He lost sight of Carrie and turned to walk towards the front of the nave, where he could see Judge Warren waiting by the chancel steps and waving at him subtly.

'All set?' Warren whispered when Jude stepped next to him. 'You look good in that suit. Nice touch.'

'All set, I think,' Jude replied in a hushed voice. 'Thank you. It belongs to Ray.'

'I know.' Warren grinned. 'Told you he was resourceful.'

The hymn finished, and silence fell upon the church. At length, Father John addressed his flock.

'Merry Christmas to you all! But please stay for another few minutes. There's something else you need to witness before you go home for your Christmas lunch.'

He raised his hands up high and lifted his head, booming out his next words. 'The Lord works in mysterious ways. And today, he has taken it upon himself to bring to us a young couple seeking to formalise their union in the eyes of God.'

A muted whisper rose from the congregation, and Jude felt himself the object of many a curious stare. He could feel an inane grin split his face nearly in half, and he didn't care. This was their moment.

The organist stepped up to the plate and launched into the bridal march. Jude's breathing grew shallow, and his ears felt as though they were full of water. He inwardly shook his head at himself. He had done God-knew how many rock concerts, some of them in sold-out arenas, but he had never experienced a sense of stage fright like this. It wasn't that he was worried about the commitment. He was terrified that he would say something dumb and let his bride down. Right at that moment, he wasn't even convinced he would be able to speak.

And then there she was, his bride. Carrie had appeared at the end of the centre aisle and was taking slow, measured steps towards him. Her face was partially obscured by the veil, but Jude knew she was smiling. He could *feel* her smile even though they were still separated by several metres of red carpet. Carrie was simply radiant.

A few steps behind Carrie, Bella followed, still carrying Maya. And behind her was Ray, wearing the biggest, most satisfied smile a man could wear.

'Uh oh,' Jude thought. 'What's he gone and done?'

Carrie reached the front of the church, and Jude lifted her veil. Carrie smiled at him, and he nearly drowned in the sea of happiness that shone out from her eyes. Why hadn't they done this sooner?

Because you're here now, and this was meant to be, a voice whispered in his head.

He took Carrie's hand, as instructed by Father John, and repeated the age-old words the minister read out to them. At least, he *hoped* he spoke. He couldn't be entirely sure because his ears had completely closed up, and all he could really hear was a dim hum of voices. It was as if he had stepped out of his body, and his mouth was acting of its own accord without any real connection to his brain. Yet whatever he said appeared to be just right, because Father John nodded contentedly and kept moving along with the ceremony.

And then, the punch line. He opened his mouth and put his every effort into speaking clearly. 'I do.'

Carrie's eyes crinkled into a smile, and her lips pursed to blow him a gentle kiss. A few seconds later, she offered her own 'I do,' and the deed was done. Almost.

'Now for the exchange of rings,' Father John prompted. 'You do have rings?'

'Um…' Jude inhaled sharply and looked for Ray. *Where are the rings?*

'Of course they do.' Ray's voice rang out, and the little Italian policeman shot forward, proffering a cushion with two rings nestling in the centre.

The minister, Jude, and Carrie stared at the offering in stunned silence for a few seconds. Jude suppressed a laugh, and he had to bite his lips so hard that he had tears in his eyes. He didn't dare look at Carrie for fear he would explode. Instead, he forced himself to breathe deeply and calmly.

'Hrrk. Hnng.' Father John cleared his throat. 'Are you ready for the exchange of rings?'

'Yes,' Jude responded before he could think twice. He took the ring that was meant for Carrie and grasped it firmly between his thumb and middle finger. Despite its size, it was surprisingly light.

Gently, he slipped the ring onto Carrie's finger while pronouncing the required words. 'With this ring, I thee wed.' He let go and examined the result. The heart-shaped rainbow-coloured plastic 'diamond' glinted on Carrie's hand, the 'stone' obscuring almost the entirety of her ring finger and the adjoining little and middle fingers. It was gaudy, it was huge, and it was utterly perfect.

He lifted his eyes to his bride's and saw that Carrie was furiously chewing her lips. Her eyes sparkled with mischief, and he understood that she, too, was trying to stop herself from bellowing with laughter.

Father John was oblivious to the undercurrent of mirth. Or if he wasn't, he did a great job pretending he was.

'And Carrie,' he prompted. Carrie nodded and took the second ring off the cushion.

'With this ring, I thee wed,' she said. She took Jude's hand and put the ring in place. Unlike hers, Jude's ring was small and dinky. It was also made of plastic, but the silver skull and crossbones looked surprisingly real. Unbelievably, the actual band had a pattern of roses embossed on it, and really, the ring couldn't have been more fitting, tacky though it was.

'I now pronounce you man and wife,' Father John concluded the improvised wedding ceremony. 'You may kiss your bride.'

Ray whooped and started clapping, followed instantly by Maria, Bella, and his entire family. Within seconds, the congregation stood and joined in. Jude shifted from foot to foot, then he lunged and planted a big kiss on Carrie's mouth. The cheering reached fever pitch, even though nobody actually knew the couple. Father John whistled and shouted, 'Merry Christmas, everyone! What a celebration we've had today.'

Jude broke off his kiss when he ran out of air, and he held onto Carrie's hands as though he was never going to let go.

Father John leaned in to whisper conspiratorially. 'I don't usually say this… You know, the "I now pronounce you man and wife" bit, or the "you may kiss the bride" bit, but it seemed fitting today. I'm glad I could be of help.'

'Thank you,' Jude said sincerely. 'Really. I can't believe we made this happen. I'm the happiest man alive.'

During this exchange, Ray's family had come forward and surrounded Carrie in a cloud of Italian well-wishers. Carrie had surrendered her bouquet and accepted her daughter back, and Maya was busy tugging at the veil.

'I think I'd better get changed back again,' Carrie laughed, 'before she ruins the dress.'

'But first we need photos,' Ray shouted above the din. 'Can't have a wedding without photos. Come on, everyone, line up.'

The rest of Christmas Day passed in rather a blur. Carrie and Jude had nary a moment to speak to each other as they got swept away by a joyous tide of seasonal and nuptial celebrations by the Italian clan that had adopted them. After a quick-fire photo session in the church, Jude and Carrie changed back into their ordinary clothes. Neither Maria nor Bella would hear of any money changing hands for dry-cleaning purposes.

'You've barely been in these clothes for half an hour,' Bella objected. 'It's nothing a good airing won't fix, don't be silly.'

If Jude had thought he would take his new wife out for lunch somewhere, he had to think again. Without even consulting them, Ray and Bella took the new Shaw family to their own home, where they extended their customary Christmas feast into an even more extensive wedding feast. The meal began with antipasto of cuts of cured meat with olives and cheese, followed by a 'surprise' *pasta al forno*. The second course brought roasted veal with potatoes and roast vegetables. Next, there was a fish course involving a seafood terrine, hot and spicy *gamberoni*, and tiny pickled anchovies. After that, Bella produced more pasta, and finally it was time to move onto the pudding, a selection of sweets and tiramisu consumed with coffee and *limoncello*.

All the family's kids and grandchildren of various ages tucked in heartily with whatever they fancied, and Carrie offered Maya small bites of pasta, mushed together potato and veal, and some of the fish. The pudding pretty much took care of itself as far as the little girl was concerned. The atmosphere was so relaxed that even at six months old, Maya was part of the action and, consequently, simply went with the flow without tantrum or hiccup.

'This is totally the way forward,' Carrie laughed towards the end of the meal. 'Although I don't think I'll ever eat again.'

'It's been perfect,' Jude concurred. 'And remember that we'll repeat the experience once we've organised the blessing ceremony. We *must* invite Ray and Bella and Maria, not least to get some of these recipes.'

'Now there's an idea,' Carrie agreed. 'Absolutely. We must!'

When all the food had been consumed and the table was cleared, everybody threatened to fall into a post-feast coma, but Ray wasn't having any of it.

'It's Christmas,' he bellowed. 'And we're celebrating a wedding. *And* there's snow. Let's go to Central Park. Let's go sledding. Build a snowman. C'mon, get your lazy butts up and let's get going.'

So amid many a good-natured protest, the entire company dressed up warm and headed out, on foot, to Central Park. It was a twenty-minute walk, give or take, and the men took turns pulling sledges that carried the younger children. There was a lot of laughing and throwing of snowballs. The skies were grey, but the snowfall had stopped. While the temperature remained well below freezing, the blizzard had come to an end.

'If it doesn't start to snow again, I'm sure the airport will be open tomorrow,' Jude whispered to Carrie. 'I'll ring later. Fingers crossed. But you know what?'

'What?' Carrie stopped walking and wrapped her arms around her husband. 'What do I know?'

'I love you. And I'm so happy you're my wife. Thank you for saying "yes".'

Carrie shook her head, smiling all the while. 'I still can't quite believe it. What a completely mad thing to do.

How utterly insane. But it's also totally magical. And okay, none of our family were here, but…'

'This is only the prelude,' Jude finished her sentence. 'I really do believe we've done the right thing, and we'll get the best of both worlds. It simply *had* to happen. It was our destiny.'

Carrie sighed happily. 'Man alive, those are big words! But I agree. There was a definite sense of fate about this. It's been absolutely magical. It's like… It's like…'

'It's a fairy tale. Our very own fairy tale in New York.'

~ 8 ~

Flying Home for Christmas

The next day broke bright and sunny over New York City. Jude rose early on Boxing Day and stood once more at the window observing the cityscape, as he had done the previous two mornings. This time, however, the sky was blue. It was bitterly cold, and the city was still covered with a thick blanket of snow, but no additional snow had fallen. The gritters and snowploughs had made good progress in clearing roads overnight. Jude fervently hoped that the situation at the airport had similarly improved.

Jude's breath formed a large circle of mist on the windowpane, and he absent-mindedly drew a love heart into it with his index finger. Smiling, he wrote a 'J' on one side and a 'C' on the other and added a cupid's arrow. He was married. Carrie was finally his wife. He was the luckiest man in the world.

'What are you doing, sweetheart?'

Carrie's voice emerged as a soft whisper from under the duvet. Jude turned and smiled.

'Morning, Mrs Shaw. How are you?'

Carrie grinned and reached out her arms to him. The resemblance to their little daughter was uncanny, and Jude's heart nearly burst with joy.

'I'm fine, thank you, *Mr* Shaw,' she quipped. 'How about you? What's the weather like?'

'Cold!' Jude shivered and jumped back into bed, cuddling up to his wife. The irony of the situation wasn't lost to him. A mere twenty-four hours earlier, a similar conversation had prompted the proposal and the ensuing wedding. How extraordinary life could be, how blessed.

'Any more snow?'

'No, no more snow. I bet we'll go home today. I'll ring the airline in a minute.'

'We have to go to the City Clerk's Office first of all,' Carrie reminded him.

'And so we shall. It opens at half past eight. We'll go there and hopefully head on straight to the airport.'

Carrie yawned and stretched lazily. 'What time is it?'

Jude consulted his watch. 'It's gone seven.'

'Babes still sleeping?'

Jude sat up and peered over into the corner where Maya was once more curled up in her drawer-cot. 'Yup.'

'Aw. Bless her. She was such a star yesterday. Not a peep out of her, no tantrum, no explosive nappies…'

'Well.' Jude laughed. 'She was the apple of Bella's eye, and all those kids kept her entertained. You know the way forward, right?'

'Errr...no. What would that be?'

Carrie yawned some more and curled back into Jude's body. He wrapped his arms around her and nuzzled his chin into her neck.

'More kids.'

'You what?'

'More kids. If they keep each other entertained, let's have six. At least.'

'Are you nuts?' Carrie protested. 'Much as I love you, but six kids? Nah. Not unless you start carrying them yourself. You know, in *your* tummy. Complete with backache and heartburn and incontinence.'

'I would, my love, I would,' Jude assured her. He meant it, too, but Carrie merely snorted.

'Easy for you to say.'

'I suppose so. But do let's have another one.'

'Okay,' Carrie relented with a smile. 'I can do one more. Or maybe two. Although we might need a little more practice first.'

Jude suppressed a laugh. 'I can do practice. As far as I'm concerned, we can practice every day.' He paused. 'We could practice right now.'

Carrie poked him in the side. 'You know we can't. Plus I'm still recovering from last night. Give a woman a break.'

Jude kissed his wife's cheek tenderly. The previous night's marital christening had been prolonged and energetic once an exhausted Maya had gone to sleep without a peep. He would cherish the moment of their first 'official' union forever.

'All right. I'll go and make some tea instead, shall I?'

'Good idea,' Carrie agreed. 'I see you're picking up rock-star *husband* qualities very quickly indeed.'

'Don't push your luck, you minx.' Jude tickled Carrie's chest and fled the bed before she could retaliate.

An hour later, the Shaw family was up, dressed, fully packed, and ready to hit the City Clerk's Office. They hadn't had breakfast, but Jude had suggested remedying that deficiency in a coffee shop or diner. The thought of a stack of pancakes with bacon and maple syrup was immensely appealing to him, and Carrie agreed.

Jude was about to summon a cab when their doorbell rang and sent them a-flutter.

'That's our doorbell,' Carrie remarked superfluously. 'What do we do?'

'I suppose we answer it,' Jude replied. 'Maybe it's Louis to take back the key.'

It wasn't Louis, but Ray. 'I'm here to get the key from you and drive you to the airport, if you need a lift,' he offered cheerfully when Jude opened the door. 'And a very good morning to you.'

'Aw, Ray. Really? Don't you have to work today?' Jude was once more overwhelmed by the little Italian's never-ending support.

'Yeah, well, I do. But my shift doesn't start until later, so I thought I'd come and say goodbye. Although it'll be weird, seeing you off. I feel like we've known each other forever. Bella is in floods of tears. She wanted to come, but there's stuff to do today.'

'We'll miss you too,' Carrie offered. 'You've all been simply amazing.'

Ray shuffled from foot to foot, then noticed their suitcases nestled by their feet.

'Y'all ready to go?'

Jude shrugged. 'Not really. I haven't been able to find out about our flights yet; the switchboards are jammed.'

Ray nodded. 'Not surprising, after two days of closure. You'll figure something out, I've got a good feeling about this. But…' he indicated their luggage. 'Where are you headed then?'

'To the City Clerk's Office, of course.' Jude grinned. 'We have to make our marriage official, don't we?'

'Of course, of course.' Ray grinned back. 'C'mon, I'll take you.'

Thus they piled once more into Ray's beloved Matilda and found themselves cruising along Lexington Avenue. Ray offered a steady commentary on the sights they were passing, and Jude marvelled yet again at the iconic views and towering buildings either side of the broad carriageway. Carrie's head turned right and left and right again as she tried to keep up with Ray's chatter, and Maya babbled along delightedly. Quite suddenly, the Chrysler Building loomed up, towered above them, and was left behind.

'What an amazing city,' Carrie sighed. 'I do wish we had more time.'

'We'll come back,' Jude assured her. 'We'll have to. Every anniversary, at least.'

'Promise?'

'Promise.'

They lapsed into silence after that. Very soon, Ray delivered them to the Marriage Bureau, where they presented themselves—in person, together, and at the same time—to file their paperwork. The clerk raised both her eyebrows at them but didn't ask any questions. Ray looked positively disappointed, Jude thought. He was certain the policeman was all set and ready to step up to their defence. In reality, his mere presence had probably facilitated matters as his name was on the paperwork.

Thirty minutes later, the deed was done. Clutching certified copies of their marriage license, the Shaw family and Ray left the building and assembled once more in Ray's car.

'Where to now?' Ray enquired solicitously.

'Breakfast?' Jude suggested before a series of beeps alerted him to an incoming text message. He retrieved his phone and broke into a grin.

'We have lift off,' he announced. 'Or we will do, soon. That was the airline. We're on the early afternoon flight. We'd better get a move on.'

'Oh hooray,' Carrie sighed. Relief was written all over her face. 'I'll miss this place, but I do want to go home.'

'Shame,' Ray opined. 'I'd better drive you over there now, though. You should check in as soon as possible.'

Jude nodded. 'Pity about the breakfast, but we'll have to find something at the airport instead.'

Ray grimaced. 'Good luck with that, but I suppose you're right. Unless…'

'Unless what?'

Ray waggled his head and dialled a number on his mobile phone. 'Yo, Alberto? *Come stai? Si.* Hey, listen, my friend, can you do me two pancakes to go please, with coffee? *Si. Si. Dieci minuti. Si. Si. Grazie.*'

He rang off and turned around, smiling at Jude and Carrie. 'Breakfast is sorted out, as long as you don't mind eating in the car.'

'Oh Ray, you're a gem,' Carrie gushed. 'Really? Are you sure? All this trouble, for us?'

'Aw, it's no trouble. Alberto's is on the way. You'll love his pancakes, and at least you'll be set for the day.'

So Ray drove them to the airport via Alberto's Little Italian Coffee Shop, where they collected a take-away breakfast 'on the house.'

'Anything is possible in New York City,' Carrie marvelled.

'Absolutely,' Ray agreed. 'You're living proof.'

A short half hour later, he deposited them at JFK airport and hugged them fiercely.

'I hate goodbyes,' he explained. 'I *will* cry. It's the Italian in me. So I'm outta here. Please stay in touch. And be safe.' He kissed Carrie on the cheek and Maya on the head before wrapping Jude in a bear hug. Swiftly, he climbed into his car and was gone.

Jude and Carrie grinned at each other and made their way to the check-in desk. Three hours later, they were airborne. Seven-and-a-half hours later, their plane touched down in Heathrow. And another hour later, the Shaw family emerged into the arrivals lounge in Terminal Five.

'There they are! Jude! Carrie!'

A barrage of greetings enveloped them as they stepped out into the vast hall. Jude skidded to a halt. Carrie laughed in disbelief.

'I don't believe it,' she whispered. 'How did they know we were arriving right now?'

'No idea,' Jude grinned and waved. A large crowd of people was waiting for them, waving 'welcome home' banners and wearing wide smiles. There were his mum and dad, Carrie's parents, some of their closest friends, all of The Blood Roses and, surprisingly, Mr Whyte.

'Wow. What a reception!' Carrie shook her head. Jude could see the pleasure shining in her eyes.

'It's amazing,' he agreed. He leaned across and whispered in Carrie's ear. 'Are we going to tell them? Or are we keeping it as a surprise a little longer?'

'Surprise,' Carrie breathed. 'It's too much to explain right here, and mum will go ballistic at having missed her only daughter's wedding.'

'There *will* be the blessing,' Jude reminded her. 'We simply need to sell her it right.'

They resumed walking to join their friends and family. Jude's mum swept Maya out of Carrie's arms and smothered the little girl in kisses. Carrie's mum did similarly with Carrie. Jude's dad hugged Jude awkwardly and took charge of the trolley. The members of The Blood Roses high-fived their lead singer and engaged in some energetic back slapping. Shouts of 'Merry Christmas' rang out left, right, and centre, and Jude was aware that their group was causing quite a commotion. He didn't care.

'Oh, Carrie, my darling, what a fiasco,' Carrie's mum complained over and above the general merriment. 'We had it all planned out. It was a disaster that you couldn't make it.'

Jude swallowed but smiled. It was always going to be Carrie's mum who would niggle and pick and complain about the inevitable.

'It was fine, Mum,' Carrie soothed her. 'It couldn't be helped.'

'But I don't understand why you didn't stick to your scheduled flight,' Carrie's mum persisted. 'You could have been home on time.'

'Ah. Well. That would be my fault,' Mr Whyte cut in from the sidelines. Jude jumped. While he had noticed the man hovering at the barrier when they first emerged, he had momentarily forgotten that he was there.

'Mr Whyte,' he beamed. 'How nice to see you again. Did you make it in time? Is everything okay?'

'I certainly did,' Mr Whyte boomed. 'And everything is fine. I have a precious little girl. She was very early, and she's still in the neo-natal unit, but she'll be fine. And my wife is doing great too. Look, here's a photo.'

He pulled out his smartphone and flipped it open. It was evident that he had already practiced the 'proud dad' routine, and Jude smiled. Carrie dutifully examined the photo and exclaimed with joy.

'She may be tiny, but she's beautiful. Congratulations, Mr Whyte. What's her name?'

'It's Peter,' Mr Whyte said, earning himself a round of confused stares. '*My* name is Peter,' he clarified. 'Her name is Suzie.'

'Ah, a good rocking name,' Jude chuckled.

'Indeed,' Peter agreed. 'Speaking of—I cannot thank you enough. If you hadn't done what you did, it could have been quite difficult. My wife… The birth wasn't easy and… Well. It was good that I was there. So thank you.'

'No problem,' Jude said. 'We had a wonderful time.'

'So I see,' Peter teased.

'What do you mean?' Jude's mum asked in a surprised tone, having listened in silence until now. 'What do you see?'

Peter looked at Jude, then at Carrie, then back at Jude.

'You haven't told them?'

'Told us what?' Now Carrie's mum was on the case too.

Peter raised an eyebrow. Jude and Carrie looked at each other. A smile tugged at Jude's mouth, and he let it bloom. 'Let's tell them,' he invited Carrie.

'Tell us *what?*' Jude's dad joined in the questioning. By way of response, Carrie very slowly lifted her hand, displaying her massively colourful wedding ring. For a minute or so, the parents and friends contemplated the meaning of her digital adornment in silent bewilderment. The Blood Roses got the meaning first and started whooping.

'You got married, man? How cool is that!'

'You got *married?*' Carrie's mum was incredulous. 'In New York? Over Christmas?'

Carrie smiled and laughed. 'We certainly did, Mum. It's a really long story. Why don't we go home, and we'll tell you there.'

'Congratulations, boy,' Jude's dad cut in, and everybody started talking at once. Jude and Carrie held hands, and Jude felt like he was floating on a cloud. What a commotion! What a fuss! What would it have been like if this clan had been at the actual wedding?

'Congratulations from me, too.' Peter pulled Jude away from the group and spoke to him earnestly. 'Honestly, you cannot believe how much it means to me that you got something special out of your calamity. I followed your adventures, you know. I knew the airport had closed and that you hadn't got on the plane. I was on the phone to the hotel the second I realised, but I was too late. I was told you'd left.'

'Well,' Jude mumbled, flustered now. 'They had no room for us.'

'So I hear. I was furious. It took some tracking down, but I heard about where you stayed. And your Santa appearance. *And* the wedding.'

'You did?' Jude was stunned. 'How?'

'I've got my sources. I thought about pulling you out of that little apartment and putting you up somewhere different, but the story was developing so powerfully, I didn't have the heart to stop it.'

'Pull us out? What *are* you talking about?' Jude frowned.

'I have my ways,' Peter said enigmatically. 'I know stuff. I have contacts pretty much everywhere. I usually get my way.'

'Who *are* you?'

'Jude? What's going on?' Carrie joined Jude and Peter and took Jude's hand. The Shaw and Collins families and the members of their band looked on, bemused, but kept their distance. Jude noticed his drummer and guitarist whispering excitedly.

'Jude?' Carrie broke into his thoughts. 'You look like you've seen a ghost.'

'Not a ghost, exactly,' Peter laughed before Jude had a chance to formulate a response. 'Here's my card.'

Jude took it. Carrie studied it over his shoulder. Jude hardly dared breathe. The card simply said, *Peter Whyte. Sound and Image*.

'You…are Peter Whyte? *The* Peter Whyte?' Jude couldn't keep a tremor out of his voice.

Peter nodded. 'That's me.'

'Oh my God. Well, I suppose that explains the suite.'

Carrie stared at Peter and Jude. 'Peter *Whyte*?'

Jude swallowed and nodded. 'Carrie, meet Peter Whyte. Executive owner at Sound and Image, a global recording label, TV and movie studio, image consultancy, and press agency. There's nothing that Peter Whyte can't do. He's, like, *the man*.'

'Wow.' Carrie breathed out sharply and spoke to Peter directly. 'I thought you looked familiar. But you seemed so normal, I never put two and two together. Of course I know you…from the telly. You're the "Talent" judge.'

Peter inclined his head. 'Yes, that too. Although that is only a small part of my business.'

'The man is a global media mogul,' Jude whispered.

Peter laughed. 'Some say that. But I do love music, and film, and television. Although music is first. Talking of which… I knew I *knew* you, back in New York. I was impressed by the fact that you didn't try to pull the rock star act on me when you thought I was a humble mortal. I've done my research. I've talked with Dan Hunter… I—'

'You what?' Jude squeaked, quite un-rock-star like. 'You talked with Dan?'

'Well, of course. He *is* your manager. I'd like to take you on. You and The Blood Roses. I'd like you to continue working with Dan, but I'd like to do your PR, your promotion. I have some ideas for a global campaign. But first and foremost, I'd like you on "The Evening Show" to tell us all about your unscheduled Christmas in New York. You, and Carrie too. Maybe even Maya, if you're agreeable.'

'You want us on "The Evening Show"?' Jude echoed.

'I certainly do.'

'Oh my God. We're *so* made,' Jude exclaimed with a huge grin.

'That's the general idea,' Peter acknowledged. 'What you did for me, and the music you make, the hard work you put in… I think you deserve a break in return.'

'Oh my gosh,' Jude reiterated, temporarily unable to string together a sentence. Carrie stepped up to the challenge on his behalf.

'He'd love to. *I'd* love to. We can tell you all about our fairy tale in New York.' She smiled.

'Fairy tale in New York, huh?' Peter grinned. 'I like that angle. But listen, it *is* still Christmas. I want you to go and enjoy the rest of the holiday with your families. I'll be in touch before the New Year. We'll make this happen. We'll make *you* happen.' He slapped Jude heartily on the shoulder.

'And the band,' Jude automatically protested. 'Not just me.'

Peter shook his head. 'And that's what I love about you, boy. You've got integrity. Yes, you *and* the band, of course. I wouldn't have it any other way. Merry Christmas!'

'Merry Christmas,' Jude replied.

'Merry Christmas, Peter, to you and your little family,' Carrie offered sincerely. She smiled, and Peter smiled in return before ambling off.

'Oh *man*.' Jude rubbed his forehead. 'Can you believe it?'

'You totally deserve this,' Carrie said steadfastly. 'You're amazing.'

'I've got to tell the band. And mum and dad.'

'And we've got to tell them all about the wedding, and you being Santa.'

'And Ray.'

'And Bella.'

'Your dress.'

'Your suit.'

Jude grinned and stared at Carrie's hand. Carrie laughed and looked at his in return.

'And these unbelievable rings,' they chorused together.

'Let's go do it,' Jude decided. 'Let's catch up on Christmas, Mrs Shaw.'

'Do let's, Mr Shaw,' Carrie beamed. 'Have I told you lately that I love you?'

'Not since we entered the UK again,' Jude complained sincerely.

'I love you, Jude.'

'I love you too, Carrie.'

'Let's roll, Jude.'

'Let's rock, Carrie.'

And so they went to celebrate a late Christmas with their families.

A few days later, Peter Whyte got in touch with Jude, as promised. Jude, Carrie, and Maya appeared on 'The Evening Show' the following week. Peter took The Blood Roses under his wing and, a year later, the band toured the world as a headlining act in their own right. But that's a different tale for another day…

Acknowledgements

First up, a huge, big, fat, enormous 'Thank You' to my readers and friends for taking part in various aspects of research for this book: Rachel Miles, for suggesting baby Maya's name; Lheanne Spicer and Tobi Helton, for advising me on Christmas hymns known (and unknown, as it were) to a North American audience; Meredith Schorr, for talking me through the geographic details of Jude and Carrie's stay; Francine LaSala, for educating me about proper street referencing etiquette; and JB Johnston, for inspiring Matilda. Evelyn Chong, Bryan Davison, Jane Risdon and Donna Morris, for remedying my lack of fluency in the Chinese language—if I got the transcription wrong, it's entirely my fault. Last but not least, huge thanks to Cameron Tilbury for adopting Ray's voice and injecting the right kind of lingo here. Awe-some!

Massive thanks to Jessie Dalrymple, who edited and test-read this manuscript with amazing speed and attention to detail, as always. I'd be lost without you, Jessie! Thanks also to my wonderful test readers, Tanya Farrell, Kelly Findlay, Jen Tucker and Meredith Schorr. I value your time and feedback more than you will ever know!

Thanks to my gorgeous husband, Jon, who, as usual kept the house ticking over and the kids entertained while mummy did her 'author thing.' Not forgetting, of course, Jon's untiring proofing efforts!

As always, I want to send big thank you hugs and smiles to all the bloggers who continue to support me with posts, shares, tweets and reviews. This goes out to you, Allyson Brann, Ana Gallardo, Andrea Coventry, Bookworm Brandee, Charlotte Foreman, Christina Torretta, Dawn Crooks, Elizabeth Santiago, Evelyn Chong, Heidi Bartlett, Inga Kupp-Silberg, Jane Hanbury, JB Johnston, Jo Hurst, Jonita Fex, Julie Ramsey, Julie Valerie, Kate Verrier, Kathleen Higgins-Anderson, Kelly Findlay, Kim Nash, Margaret Literary Chanteuse, Melanie Robertson-King, Melissa Amster and the whole team at Chick Lit Central, Nicole Henke, Rosie Amber, Samantha March, Sharon Goodwin, Simona Elena, and Stephanie Oursler.

And of course YOU. Thank you for reading and for your continued interest in my authorly journey. I write for you, because that's what I do. I love to hear from you, so don't hesitate to get in touch via Facebook or Twitter or by email at nickywells@yahoo.co.uk. Rock on!

About the Author

Ultimate rock chick author Nicky Wells writes romance with rock stars—because there's no better romantic hero than a golden-voiced bad boy with a secret soft heart and a magical stage presence!

Nicky's books offer glitzy, glamorous romance with rock stars—imagine Bridget Jones *ROCKS* Notting Hill! If you've ever had a crush on any kind of celebrity, you'll connect with Nicky's heroes and their leading ladies.

Born in Germany, Nicky moved to the United Kingdom in 1993 and currently lives in Lincoln with her husband and their two boys. Nicky loves listening to rock music, dancing, and eating lobsters. When she's not writing, she's a wife, mother, occasional knitter, and regular contributor at Siren 107.3 FM with her own monthly show. Rock on!

Join Nicky on her blog at http://nickywells.com/ or on Twitter, Facebook, Goodreads, Pinterest and Google+.

Also by Nicky Wells

Sophie's Turn (Rock Star Romance Trilogy, Part 1)

Sophie's Run (Rock Star Romance Trilogy, Part 2)

Sophie's Encore (Rock Star Romance Trilogy, Part 3)

Spirits of Christmas ~ A Rock'n'Roll Christmas Carol

Fallen for Rock

NICKY WELLS

Coming from Nicky Wells in 2015

Seven Years Bad Sex

One wedding. One cursed mistake. Disaster ever after?

A seven-years-bad-sex curse? Surely not! However, *something* went wrong when rock singer Casey and drummer Alex got married on that beautiful yacht anchored off St Tropez in the south of France. Something went *badly* wrong. For even on their wedding night, the young couple discovers a complete and somewhat surprising inability to make love. Muddling through their honeymoon with a string of thin excuses for their predicament, the lovers defer finding a solution (and panicking) until the return to their home in London. After all, they married for life and to make rock music, not for the love of sex. Right?

Yet when they resume life as normal in London, all hell breaks loose. Increasingly frantic in their quest for release, the unhappy newlyweds embark on a string of hilarious and occasionally harmful antics that drives them, their band, and an assortment of random strangers to the brink of despair. But it ain't over 'til it's over or, in this case… it ain't over 'til the newlyweds sing.

Printed in Great Britain
by Amazon

34049025R00088